Reade

I immediately thought that if I met Nancy Camden, we would be instant friends. I look forward to future work.

Deborah Cullen
Lewisburg, West Virginia

It made us laugh out loud. Excellent character development. We found we couldn't put it down.

Jon and Patricia Hecker
Spencer, Indiana

After I got into it, I found it hard to put down. It's an interesting, different third person way of presenting a story.

June Mork
Renville, Minnesota

While I would not want any of these characters in my home, I felt compassion and interest in them because they were richly developed.

Ann Green , D.A.
Brooklyn, Michigan

I felt as though I was getting the *true story*, the inner life of people I've known. It was a good encapsulation of life from the mundane to the profound. I can't wait for her next book.

Lawrence Sanders
Milwaukee, Wisconsin

ThE True Story
of
Jimmy TruEberry

A Novel
by
Nancy Camden

Cover Photo & Book Design
by
Nancy Camden

Raspberry Hill Press
Horton, Michigan

Inquiries should be addressed to
Raspberry Hill Press
P.O. Box 73
Horton, MI 49246

Library of Congress Catalogue Number: 98-091502
Camden, Nancy
The True Story of Jimmy Trueberry
ISBN 0-9664930-0-1

Printed by an employee owned company
on recycled acid-free paper with soy inks.

FIRST EDITION

To Mary Hauser

ThE True Story
of
Jimmy TruEberry

A Novel

One

Jimmy Trueberry's big old New Yorker with balding tires loses momentum halfway up Cindy Mead's long steep driveway. Yellow and rust, it lunges forward several times in fitful jerks only to slide back farther. It flails its rear end from side to side flashing brake lights as though it is throwing a tantrum—wedged between a climb and a slide.

When Jimmy finally realizes his New Yorker isn't going any farther, he gives up and shoves the shift lever into park. Frustration pounds on the steering wheel in time to the music on 99.2 as The Motor City's "Take-A-Hike Mike" spews irreverence to the delight of his teenage audience across the state. Like a parent raptor he deposits his carrion into the throats of open-beaked, angry little heavy-metal vultures. Here in Reed County, Jimmy isn't feeding on Take-A-Hike's words. He's in a primitive feeding frenzy of the beats that pulsate from the speakers, fusing his mind to what he's about to give Mrs. Cindy Mead.

Inside her little house on the hill, Cynthia Wickett Mead is draped in a chair at the big round table oblivious to the impending invasion of her staged scenario. Cindy has closed the curtains. She needs darkness to express what she's feeling—a wilting, dying-on-the-vine, poison ivy mood that dominates her almost daily.

At the big electrical spool that Bruce made into a table seventeen years ago, Cindy Mead's finger pokes at the uncomfortably hot wax dripping from a hand-dipped candle onto a handmade ceramic plate. Artificial pine scent from the candle is the closest this house will get to a Christmas tree. This youth-of-the-sixties won't participate in the growing and killing of a spruce or a pine just so she can have a dying tree loaded with pesticides in the house for a few weeks in December.

She's not into cheer. Not now. Not ever—except for that one year which has been over for several months. Besides, there are no children to demand Christmas; so, who cares?

Out in his car, Jimmy focuses on his mission when the pulsating on the radio changes for a hyper commercial. Pumped up, he turns the ignition key nipping "Take-A-Hike" midsentence and reaches for the plastic K-Mart sack on the front seat—the bag that has been riding around in Jimmy's car for weeks while Jimmy worked up his nerve. Today's the day! Jimmy Trueberry has skipped Math to unload on this Mead woman.

The snow on the ground is heavy and wet—slick! A few more degrees and last night's snow would have been rain. Jimmy slams the car door, leans forward and sloshes up the drive.

Cindy looks at the kitchen clock. Her mood darkens another shade. Bruce will be home in an hour. She has to get those dishes washed. Evidence. He'll be able to look at them and see that she's been eating all day. She has to find something she can point to that will falsely account for productivity. After all, he has to work, while she "lays around the house doing nothing." Those are his exact words. What Bruce doesn't understand is that Cindy has never in her life done nothing. Even when she looks like she's doing nothing, she's thinking and that's not the same as nothing. Someday, she believes, all of this thinking is going to pay off. "Thinking" without immediate, identifiable financial reward is valueless according to Bruce. Cindy never runs to Bruce to show him a new painting. She always runs to wave the check for it and he says, "Now *that,* that looks good."

Cindy imagines herself at a New York gallery show opening of her paintings. Sophisticated people are milling about looking comfortable with wine glasses in their hands, oohing and ahhing over her "provocative" work. Cindy basks in the ambiance, the praise, the power to snub the people on the list she's accumulated since childhood . . . until in her imagination, she spots Bruce pasted to the wall in his standard plaid shirt and jeans over by the hors d'oeuvre table, slurping from a wine glass wishing it were beer, sneaking side looks, emanating a combination of suspicion and disgust.

When Jimmy reaches the garage at the top of the hill, he stops to peek in the window of an overhead garage door. One bay is empty. In the middle bay is Cindy's Ford pickup and in the bay closest to the house is a black and chrome jewel—a Harley Hog that looks to Jimmy like its never been ridden. Jimmy's Uncle Skin had a wrecked Hog, but he isn't his uncle any more. Maybe never was. Jimmy's dad doesn't believe that Aunt Sis and Skin ever made it legal.

The Mead's house is built into the ground on two sides on this lower level. Most people would classify it as small and plain. Jimmy sees posh. He approaches a green door on the walk out side. There he steps into a mirror. Jimmy Trueberry a.k.a. Dack Dick (his secret second psyche super hero who's in a hot band) reflect back in the door window as though Jimmy and Dack were on the inside of Cindy Mead's house looking out at their overlapping selves.

Jimmy grasps the plastic bag with the big red "K" tightly to his chest with both hands like a Christian clutching his bible on judgment day. Suddenly his vision is lost in the blur of his crisis.

Upstairs Cindy passes her finger through the flame of the candle. Her eyes well up with tears. She takes a deep breath and exhales it as a long whine. Thinking. Again.

Bruce spews at her regularly, "You think too much!" Like her brain has a valve that can turn it on and off. When Bruce's head hits the pillow, he's snoring in five minutes. Cindy is laying there—thinking—listening to his snores, unable to toss or turn because that disturbs Bruce who has been in bed since around nine. If it goes on too long, Cindy ice skates.

. . . she and he glide around and around a big ice rink, in an empty stadium, dramatically penetrated by a moving shaft of pink light. Her fuchsia colored chiffon skirt pulsates in the cool breeze, limp against the force of air. A smattering of silver sequins glisten and shine in droplets at the neck opening of her leotard. They glide, she and he. His name is Demetri. Her name is Portia. She is young, athletic, smug about being blonde and having such a cool name. She is held firmly by Demetri. As he skates her backward, her hands feel the hardness of his body. He guides Portia back. She trusts him, fully. They skate as one. They gain speed. As they round a corner, his steel blade digs into the ice, scraping across the smooth surface creating a fine spray of little crystals that looks like shattered glass. At the same moment, he cups his hands around her tiny

*waist and easily lifts her into the air above
his head. Up there, her chiffon skirt flaps
against the air like the wings of a bird. Flap,
flap, flap! Her warm skin tingles as her body
slices against the crisp air. Up there her
body is rigid, parallel to hard ice. Her head
is light, her vision foggy, her breathing
shallow, her heart pounding. She can't tell if
she is hovering above or beneath. She raises
her arms slowly and gracefully like a
ballerina, her long fingers reach out, out,
until, until . . .*

Bink! The rink will disappear. The pink shaft of light will
disappear. Demetri will disappear and she can't get any of
it to come back for more than a flash. (Demetri will only
come once a night.) So, without choice, Cindy will lie in bed
thinking herself down a more dull path for another fitful
night.

She might think about where Bruce would put a new storage
shed for the lawn mower. Then she might contemplate
whether she will be able to stand having it there . . . or she
might think about what Phil Donahue is really like and if he
and Marlo are really happy together since Marlo was single
for all of those years. Even though it looks like a match
made in heaven, Cindy regularly wonders, is any match made
in heaven? Of course, Cindy's marriage was—made in heaven.
For nearly twenty years that was her cherished illusion.

Looking at the window's glass reflection, Jimmy squints and
focuses on his blue-tinted face. He's trying to see if Charlie
is hidden there in his eyes, brown and almond shaped or his
broad nose or is he right there on the surface blasting out at
everyone, but seen by no one because who would be looking
for Charlie Yates in Jimmy Trueberry's face.

5

Cindy sits at the table with her eyes closed, lids fluttering slightly. She thinks of Phil Donahue. Linda, her sister-in-law has read his autobiography. She told Cindy that they called him little Philly when he was a kid.

Every day Cindy listens to or tapes little Philly, Oprah, and Sally Jesse. Bruce complains that the TV is always on, even though it's not upstairs where Cindy watches it, but in Cindy's studio where she creates her paintings while people tell their stories. Some artists paint to jazz or classical music or god forbid (Cindy can't believe this) silence. Cindy paints to talk shows: Too Fat to be a Cheerleader; Stripper Grandmas on this edition of . . . ; *Today,* Career Women Who Can't *Commit* and Their Mothers Who Crave Grandchildren; *Tomorrow,* For Forty-Five Years, They Called Him Joe, Now They Call Him Jennifer.

Suddenly big red lips come into focus as Jimmy's face disappears. Big red lips on the face of a bare-breasted, bare-naked woman's body. Jimmy cups his hand beside his eye and presses his face to the glass. The room is filled with pictures of buck-naked women. Huge pictures almost as tall as Jimmy are propped up around the room—not camera pictures but artist pictures. "Wow!" Jimmy whispers. The women in the paintings are strangely distorted, big trunks, small breasts, and big red lips. Most of them are reclining on something—an old-fashioned sofa, a dull brown wooden floor. One of them is floating on her back between two trees with identical black cats on every branch.

Is anybody really normal or happy? Cindy wonders as she runs her palm across the table top! She has her doubts about those who might profess it. They must have some big denial going about the reality of their life which it seems can be sustained indefinitely. Oprah's always referring to the Queen-of-de-Nile. Cindy recalls the woman on Oprah's show yesterday whose husband, a respected ophthalmologist in a small town in Kansas had secretly hypnotized some of his female patients as they looked at the eye chart through that big contraption and then had taken about twice as long to give them the "eye" exam in a locked examination room while his wife answered the phone across the hall, made appointments and took Tupperware orders. "Tupperware was my avocation," she had revealed to Oprah and the nation as she sat up straight in her chair for the first time since the show began and had rambled on about a new blue party-tray with lid. Cindy could tell she had wanted to turn *The Oprah Winfrey Show* into a national Tupperware party instead of what it was that day—a national exposé on her husband's sexual perversion.

Didn't she have an inkling that her old Doc was in there handling some things he shouldn't before he finally got busted by the Chief of Police's busty, new, third wife who'd volunteered to go undercover and get her eyes examined to dispel the rumors of wrongdoing but had to end up *pretending* when he tried to hypnotize her? "She ain't susceptible, no ma'am, not to hypnotism!"

Recounting how old Doc McMullen had unbuttoned her blouse and tried to fondle her breasts, Lynette had told the audience, "I screamed first and then made a citizen's arrest, slapping handcuffs on him. I'm goooooood with handcuffs." Lynette informed the world. At that, Cindy remembers, she lost the grip on her paint brush.

Old Mrs. McMullen had professed on *Oprah* that she believes in her husband and believes he was set up by the dozen women who believe *they* are the victims. Mrs. McMullen had talked via a satellite hookup from Kansas because the Doc who is in the state prison is ailing and she didn't want to go too far away or miss a visit *and* because she, quote—would not sit in the same studio with that blonde B-I-T-C-H if my life depended on it. My husband is not a molester—unquote. Then she exclaimed with half-cured cement firmness that those women were sex-starved, and they were after her husband. That's what Mrs. McMullen had said she believes as she sat there on national TV, blue-haired, while the blonde B-I-T-C-H punched the air with her acrylic nails and with a cocky, husky cigarette voice said, "She's right, Oprah, he's *not* a *molester,* he's a *convicted molester*—a *fat, bald, ugly, old convicted molester.*" With that the audience expressed themselves with a smattering of applause and a lot of oohing captured by the cameras.

Cindy's thoughts turn to Bruce who is always wrinkling up his nose as he passes through the studio on the lower level which used to be a two-car garage. Bruce gets one or two lines of somebody's story or sees a row of obese people on sofas talking about how *it can't be helped.* Boy, he hates it when fat people claim that. Bruce had lost forty pounds before he met Cindy and has kept it off all of these years. He knows that all it takes is willpower, damn it! Without ever stopping for an answer, Bruce has asked many times as he passes through the studio, "Why do you want to hear about all of those weird people's depressing lives?"

Now or never, Jimmy thinks as he clutches the bag which holds the whole depressing story that brought him to this point in his life where he will unload on Cynthia Wickett Mead. His fist is raised to the door. He knuckle raps it five, six, seven times.

I'm looking at *life,* Cindy explains to herself upstairs in her house. She often says that to Bruce after he comments on her talk show habits as he walks through the studio on his way to the garage. Most of the time she ends up saying it to no one. Bruce never stops in the studio for any reason.

If she could get the story straight from the horse's mouth she would, except everyone is so damn secretive until they get on a TV talk show before millions of viewers. I simply want to know what's really going on around me, Cindy tells herself.

When no one comes to the green painted door, Jimmy prowls around for another door. He finds himself at the other end of the cedar board-and-batten house where there are several cords of split firewood stacked under an awning that is attached to the house. On a rust colored door he vigorously knocks three times, biting his upper lip while his eyes lower to focus on tiny mouse tracks in a dusting of snow (that looks like tiny crystals) that has blown under the awning and onto the cement walkway.

Jimmy presses his face to the glass. Shop tools are scattered about the basement, power tools—a band saw, two table saws, a drill press, router, belt sander, shelves with a circular saw and other things with cords. "Travis could sell this stuff, easy," Jimmy notes, talking out loud to himself, "if he weren't in the juvie."

The chair under Cindy groans as she shifts her weight. Bruce hates these wooden, Victorian chairs at the table because they're fragile and always falling apart, coming unglued. Bruce hates that. Bruce hates hassles and complications. He's got enough to do to get himself to work everyday while Cindy "fools around at home" instead of being the teacher her parents paid umpteen hundreds of dollars for, like Bruce's dad who expected him to be a teacher and he is, even though he hates the paperwork and the administrative hassles. It's always some hassle, he repeatedly explains to Cindy as she mentally dances on umpteen eggshells.

Jimmy follows the tiny mouse footprints out from under the awning to the south part of the house where he sees a stairway leading to an upper level deck at the *front* of the house, even though he thinks he's at the *back*. Anyone would think it until they get inside.

Before Jimmy was born, when this house was being built, people around here assumed that the Mead's house was facing the normal way—toward the road. Everyone assumed it until the Mead's neighbor, Bernice Spurr, discovered otherwise and spread the news on the grapevine—"those hippies up there in the trailer on the hill are building their house to face the wrong way." The Mead's were oblivious to observation, clucking tongues, scratched heads. They'd claimed isolation. They had no idea they were under neighborhood watch, victims of drive-by viewings from creeping cars whose occupants were peeping between the tree trunks for glimpses of the new people's stuff so they could get them properly categorized in an informal rural who's who.

From his kennel Buster Beagle's pop-eyes have discovered Jimmy, poking around the deck, but he doesn't bark. Buster's bark hurts his ears and makes him involuntarily shake his head after each one. He uses it for real *threats*— like roaming dogs, Jimmy's dad and hot air balloons. When the wind blows this direction from town during Reedville's Hot Air Jubilee, balloons have floated over vocalizing deep whooshing sounds. Something Buster has never forgotten. That is why his eyes roll up every once in a while.

Right now Buster's eyes are riveted to Jimmy's back searching to find an eye for contact as he nervously prances in place, sniffing to catch a scent to identify the familiar form. Buster needs the forms help—help getting back in the house where he can belly up on that warm, soft rug in the middle of the room. The white tip of his tail wags like a truce flag on a stick. "Peace!" it screams, furiously. "Peace, please!" Buster's been put out for eating cat poop from the litter pan *again*, and for topping that by puking it up on Cindy's hand made room-sized, braided blue jeans rug that must be professionally cleaned and fell apart both times it was. Buster knows he's in deep BAD. She had repeated it over and over, fast and harsh, high pitched at first, pointing her finger at him and the barf and back to him. Then, she had put her hands on her hips, puffing herself up like Buster when his fur stands up on his back. The big alpha dog had droned "BAAAAAD" several more times deep and drawn out. Buster had cowered when she asked if he wanted to go to the penitentiary. He'd pasted his tail between his legs, crawled on his belly, tried to hide. Did everything he could to look ashamed, but he still had to do time in the pen.

Oblivious to Buster, Jimmy is facing a big blue door, a more imposing one that doesn't have a window. Dack Dick puts his ear to the door, listens for a few seconds, cracks his knuckles and announces to himself, "Somebody's in there!"

What he thought he heard was a siren. Somebody's in there watching *Rescue 911* Jimmy decides—even though it's only two o'clock, Thursday. Jimmy Trueberry knows you can't tell the time or the day of the week from hearing television. Sometimes late at night when he sneaks downstairs to call his friend, who's real cool and has got it made—her name is Starr—she's playing the daytime soap, *Days of our Lives* on her own VCR in her bedroom.

Jimmy understands why nobody is opening the door. He wouldn't come either during *Rescue 911*—even if it were on tape which it wouldn't be at his house because his old man doesn't believe those "damn machines" are necessary and wouldn't let one in his house even if they got it free—just like Jimmy's granpap Trueberry wouldn't let a TV set in *his* house and like *his* dad before *him* wouldn't get a phone. *Nobody* in the Trueberry family *gets* until everybody else has long *got*. Sometimes they never get at all. The Trueberry descendants are obstinate. They call it independent.

The only reason they have a TV is so Jimmy's old man, Eugene can watch *Michigander's Outdoor Life* on Wednesday nights at eight. He used to be against TV until after Eugene's dad died and his brother-in-law Kink relented and let Eugene back in his house. It was at Kink's where Eugene was seduced by TV. Eugene's favorite Wednesday of the year is when *Outdoor Life* features "Big Buck Bonanza." That's the show that made him lust after Kink's TV.

"Big Buck Bonanza" is when the closest thing to John Wayne (in Eugene's estimation), Howard "Big Mac" Lewiston gives shiny, silver trophies and gift certificates for antler racks with the most and longest tines and the biggest spread. On "Big Buck Bonanza," "Big Mac" shares with the viewers fuzzy snapshots of posing, grinning hunters in neon orange jackets and hats, holding up (for the snapshot) the heads of gutted deer with glassy eyes, tongues hanging out, strung up by their back legs from trees. "Tell me now, ain't that just a beaut?" an excited "Big Mac" proclaims every year and Eugene (he-man hunter) shouts back at the screen that they truly are just about the most beautiful pictures he can imagine. When Jimmy witnesses "Big Buck Bonanza" in his living room, it reminds him of being at his ma's holy roller Pentecostal church on an exceptionally spiritful Sunday.

Throughout the show, when he gets excited, "Big Mac" throws his bushy, silver-haired head back and howls like a wolf. It's his trademark. Jimmy's dad gets the biggest kick out of that—how "Big Mac" seems to enjoy making such an ass out of himself with that OW, OW, OOOOOOW.

Nearly every week since they got the TV, ten years ago, Eugene, Jimmy and Will, Jimmy's older brother, have watched *Michigander's Outdoor Life* together. During the annual worship at the alter of "Big Buck Bonanza," there has been a father/son communion with slices of spicy deer sausage from the freezer piled high on Ritz wafers. But no more. Several months ago, Eugene chased Will out of the house with the wood stove poker, driving him off to Indiana to his fat granny's hairy arms.

Thinking of Will makes Jimmy's head feel heavy. He leans against the door.

Cindy pulls at the little pouch of skin under her chin that she swears looks more gross every day. She's been purging this afternoon—that's her thing lately, an emotional *purge* that includes some babbling about her life, expressed with a whole lot of loud crying that comes from deep inside and explodes in high pitched wailing out her mouth. There's forty-one years suppressed down there but for several months now Cindy's been ritually letting out more than she's been stuffing down. Cindy's changing, privately. Green wax pools at the top of the candle as she snatches a fresh Kleenex from the box. She feels herself welling up—*toxic people, codependency, contagious emotions, family secrets, denial, industrial strength dysfunction in bulk* emerging from the pit of her being. Her heart pounds, hurts, actually hurts. The pain is on its way . . . on its way . . . on its way. Cindy's mouth opens real wide but not very tall, her eyes close and then, BOOM! Out bursts another shrill, "yeeeeeeeeeeeeeeeeeeeee!"

"Alllllll right!" Jimmy says as he hears the shrill siren again, starting low and building in volume. Jimmy loves *Rescue 911*. He'll never forget the one where, after doing show-off dives in a Florida River, a kid got attacked by an alligator. Jimmy loved it when everybody in the simulation jumped up and down on the dock, waving their arms and hollering about seeing an alligator. The kid who couldn't hear what they were yelling, grinned from ear to ear relishing his "awesomeness" until he found himself in the grin of a gator. Jimmy couldn't tell if in the simulation, they used a fake boy with a real gator or a real boy with a fake gator. Of course, it could have been a fake gator *and* a fake boy. However they did it, man, it was cool. Jimmy thinks that the best thing about *Rescue 911* is knowing that the victims in the stories survive—even if they're crippled for life which they rarely show. They never do stories where people die. Jimmy doesn't want to see that—he's seen dying for real.

Jimmy takes to drumming the palms of his hands on Cindy Mead's blue door. He couldn't stop it if he tried. Pounding rhythm on things happens when Dack Dick is inspired and he's truly inspired hearing the siren on *Rescue 911* through Cindy Mead's front door.

"eeeeeeeee . . . !!" Cindy Mead stops vocalizing mid-wail. Her mouth gapes open taller than wide. "Damn!" she says snapping it shut, both hinges cracking as usual. "Who the hell is that?" When the pounding on the front door stops the house is silent, except for a whining Fridgidaire Elite that's also been expressing itself lately. Whir, rat, rat! Whir, rat, rat! Cindy goes over and hits it up the side. "Run-down piece-of-crap," she hisses. The whining stops. It's twenty years old and dying like the other twenty year old things around her.

Cindy doesn't unlock *any* door, blindly, to anyone. The trailer court where she and Bruce had lived their first year of marriage was by the prison's trustee camps and until they clamped down, prisoners were all the time walking away. You still read about it happening every once in a while in the paper. There was a prison breakout at "The World's Largest Walled Prison" that was down the road nearer to town. The escape with a helicopter landing in the prison yard was made into a movie. There's a sign out on the interstate near town that says: "Do not pick up hitchhikers." The next sign announces rather defensively: "Reedville—*We* like it here!"

Cindy stomps in her stocking feet down the hall to the bathroom window on the same side as the front door. She steps up on the toilet lid, pulls back the curtain, quietly slides open the inside wooden frame and presses her right cheek against the cold storm window to get a view back down to the other end of the house.

Jimmy is down there with his ear stuck to her door, picking at his nose, stomping the snow off his hi-tops onto the deck. Jimmy's lips are moving but Cindy can't see anyone with him. Cindy pulls her cheek off the glass leaving a cold, red circle on her face and a smudge on the glass that she may clean off, someday.

It's that shit-ass kid, she realizes. Cindy looks at herself in the mirror avoiding looking directly at her face. If she looks at her face she'll never recover—never while she's in this mood. With her selective vision, she focuses on the hair. It becomes a halo around a nonexistent face. "Damaged," she says jabbing angrily at her recently permed, highlighted, shoulder length hair. It passes through her mind that she should think about changing her style to something more rebellious. Maybe she should go with damaged as an art form—spiked, orange, shaved up the sides. After all she *is* an artist and aren't all true artists damaged, untamed? Her hair is like this to please her Bruce. But *what about Cindy?* She find's herself asking that a lot, as though Cindy were some other person for whom she is pleading a case. "Ladies and gentlemen of the jury," asks the defense, "what about Cindy?" She asks herself that all of the time in the courtroom inside her mind where there has been a trial of some kind in progress for as long as she can remember.

Cindy blows her nose on a piece of North Winds toilet paper. Several months ago Cindy had made an abrupt announcement to Bruce that she *never* liked the brand of toilet paper that Bruce has been buying for nearly twenty years. She had argued that it doesn't hold together very well and balls up. According to Bruce this was a ball out of left field. He's got a lot of sensitivity back there. This is an important issue to him and he considers himself a bit of an expert. He made it clear that this is the brand he's settled on and he's not about to mess himself up experimenting

He said he couldn't understand why after all these years— why its become such an issue with Cindy. Why everything has become an issue. Besides as he tells her over and over, it's *his* money that buys all of the groceries and *he* does all of the shopping because *he* does all of the cooking. It's like he always says, *"You want it done right—you do it yourself"* and he always does. If Cindy were to get a compromise on this toilet paper issue, it would be Bruce telling her she may buy her own brand and keep it on the back of the toilet.

15

They have separate just about everything else. Much of it has always been separate from day one. Separate checking accounts, separate bank loans, separate TV antennas (one for upstairs and one for her TV in the studio), separate parcels of land within their twenty acres paid for separately on which they submit separate checks for each of their share of the property tax. Now they have separate meals at the same time at the same table. Cindy is just beginning to suspect that she and Bruce might be—she can hardly bring herself to think it—might be . . Oh, god . . . . *separating!*

Cindy got real testy around her fortieth birthday, announcing a lot of things. Like she didn't like the way Bruce cooks. Then she had gone one further and opined that she could be a better cook, maybe even a gourmet cook, which Bruce had mocked repeatedly saying "gourmet" like it looks on paper, "gur-met." Cindy had told Bruce that she was tired of Campbell's mushroom soup or tomato bisque soup (which he pronounces "bis-cue") in *everything*. Although Bruce is tired of all of the responsibility, he's not about to give up the reins on anything precisely because of the first dish Cindy cooked after her pronouncement. It was an Indian curry with rice and strong spices (savage to Bruce's intestines) and sliced "bananas" on top (Bruce couldn't believe that). Bruce knew Cindy was pretending that she was relishing every mouthful.

Bruce had sniffed at that curry for what had seemed like a couple of years to Cindy. She had watched him in her peripheral vision. Then Bruce got up and had made himself a whole other meal which put his eating about an hour off schedule. He had to warm some canned mixed vegetables. He'd made Betty Crocker Potatoes Au Gratin with Campbell's mushroom soup to *zip* it up, and he'd fried a pack of tofu which he'd smothered in soy sauce. According to Cindy there is at least one dish every day smothered in soy sauce. Soy sauce á la chow mein. Soy sauce á la burritos. Soy sauce á la spaghetti. Cindy thinks Bruce should do a cookbook,

16

Around the World with Soy Sauce. The one thing they *share* is that neither one of them eats meat, but of course, for different reasons—Cindy for ethical reasons and Bruce because of his sensitive intestines.

One day Bruce had decided that two could play this power game. So without announcement—Bruce does *not* display theatrics—he'd begun doing his own laundry. For years, to no avail, he'd been complaining about the way Cindy does laundry. Now that he does it, he bleaches his underwear every week. Cindy never bleaches. She worries about the environment. Bruce worries about germs and the stains in his jockey shorts.

For twenty years Cindy had insisted on hanging their laundry on lines—lines outside or on the enclosed porch or the lines that were strung from support beam to support beam across the living room. Cindy has worried for years about energy consumption. In the winter wet clothes added moisture to the dry air of a wood-heated house—a more environmentally sound solution than a humidifier. She didn't think of it as the "hillbilly" thing to do. She thought of it as the "right" thing to do.

Bruce brought home a dryer three months ago and a humidifier. The clothes are softer now. The towels and jeans don't stand up by themselves like they did when they were line dried. Cindy is secretly happy about that dryer. It has made her life a lot easier. Still, she feels as though a chapter in her life has been lost. The sixties—gone.

Bruce thinks that Cindy is menopausal. Cindy knows that! *Something* hormonal is happening. She's finding course white hairs in her eyebrows and starting a beard with one persistent white hair on her chin. Bruce thinks she's frigid. Cindy used to think that, too. But, as of a year ago, Cindy discovered otherwise.

She gives her nose one last blow and heads for the door. There is another knock before she gets there. Cindy twists the lock. As she turns the doorknob, she feels a resistance on the other side of the knob. The-kid-has-hold-of-her-doorknob. An uncontrollable surge of irritation rushes through Cindy. Quietly, but with intensity she says to herself, as she raises one eyebrow, "Let it go, boy." She says it the way she would say it if she were Bette Davis acting in a dramatic movie, her red-nailed fingers wrapped around the barrel of a young punk's loaded gun pointed at her as she tries to convince him to give it up. Well, it *is* a dramatic moment. Cindy's about to face "shithead," and by god he *isn't* going to throw anything at her this time. She simply couldn't take it.

Cindy throws her head back and opens the door in a big, dramatic sweeping motion á la Betty Davis as one of those strong, bitchy women. Cindy lays the house wide open as if to say, "You don't scare me, punk!" Cindy thinks it would be so neat to have a long cigarette holder for moments like these when she needs a symbol of haughty superiority, even though she doesn't smoke.

Jimmy Trueberry is planted at her blue door under a farmer's cap advertising Decalb seed corn. He's a little taller than the last time. The whites of his eyes have a pink cast—like Cindy's. His angular face is a field of puffy little abscesses in various stages of eruption just like his life which has ushered him for the third time straight into Cindy's. Cindy is *not* smiling as she folds her arms and leans her right shoulder onto the door frame and says, "Yeah?"

Jimmy bends over to pick up the plastic K-Mart bag that is crumpled beside his feet. He clutches it tightly in front of him.

Poor baby! Poor Jimmy's cold, Cindy thinks as she notices him shivering in an unbuttoned, stiff jeans jacket that isn't even close to being warm enough for the winter temperatures.

Cold air rushes past Cindy into the house. Earlier she opened a window trying to cool things down before Bruce arrived home to lecture her about waste. The litany: She doesn't appreciate what it takes to work all week and then to cut and split wood on the weekends. She doesn't appreciate how he keeps a year ahead because wood must dry properly before it's burned.

Their closest neighbor, Mike Spurr cuts, splits, and burns his as needed from week to week and as a result has a big, patched crack in his chimney. Rita Spurr envies Cindy for their mound of wood. Cindy is religious about warmth in the winter. She can't help but appease herself, oversacrificing wood to the furnace. She knows it's wasteful but she can never get warm enough in the winter. She even gets up every night for the three am feeding so the fire doesn't go out before morning.

The kid is shifting his weight quickly now from hi-top to hi-top, almost jogging in place. The first time Cindy laid eyes on him he was about four years old. She's pretty sure that's who it was since he was practically in the Trueberry's yard. Two little kids were hiding in some brush on a little knoll beside the road. It was late fall and most of the leaves had already dried up and dropped off, so Cindy could easily see the hunkered figures. They were wearing knit caps—maize and blue. She knew it was maize and not garish gold because around here, that color with blue means you're a University of Michigan Wolverine fan. Maize and blue. That's one of the first things Cindy learned when she became a Michigander. She also learned how to hold up her right hand, fingers extended, palm facing out and point to where Reedville is located on the palm of her hand which became a map in the shape of the lower peninsula of Michigan. Reedville is at the bottom of her lifeline.

Just as Cindy drove by the knoll that day years ago, the smaller figure had stepped out of the brush and heaved a rock at Cindy's first Ford truck—which she'd only had three weeks. Boy, was she pissed! She had *thought* she heard it hit, but it could have been a bump in the music—it had a kind of heavy bass.

"I heard you write stories," Jimmy blurts out as he runs his finger under his nose and then across his jeans leg.

Cindy glares at Jimmy and wonders how it is that everybody knows everybody else's business around here. All she did was mention to Rita Spurr that she was taking Creative Writing over at Reedville Community College. Cindy is *not* a writer! Cindy suspects that Rita thinks she's peculiar and making her out to be a writer is one more way of pointing out how peculiar she is. She can hear it now. "A writer! Just *what* does she write?"

One summer when Cindy grew tomatoes in pots on her deck, Rita had acted funny when she saw them. Cindy thinks that Rita had suspected they were marijuana plants until she got a closer look. (The marijuana was in the woods.) But even when she'd figured out they were tomato plants, Rita had acted as though Cindy was doing something illegal. The problem was and still is that with twenty acres of land, the only flat, treeless spot on the twenty is over the septic tank and you can't grow food there! Rita's house is on a big flat piece of land. Big Mike had bulldozed it flat so there is plenty of room for a garden and a go-cart track that circles the house for little Mike who races around that house for hours.

There's a grapevine out in this neck of the county that spreads the word about things that Cindy thinks should mean *nothing* to these people. It's an old grapevine with tendrils that curl around people with roads named after their ancestors and others who through some nebulous rite have proved themselves *local*. (Whenever Cindy says *local*, she pronounces it *loco*. When she refers to the historical society, she calls it the Loco Hysterical Society.) It's the same loco vine that Mike Spurr's mother was connected to when she lived in the shacky house in which Mike was raised. (He bulldozed it down when they got the new house built fifteen feet from the old.)

Twenty years ago when Cindy and Bruce had moved their trailer to the property Mike's mom, Bernice, had come puffing up the hill to deliver a frozen pie, uncooked Swanson's Cherry with frost caked on the waxy box an inch thick. She had come to find out how things were going to be up here on the hill—to determine if they were going to be affecting her down there. Her dog, Blackie had come up with Bernice to sniff Cindy's dog, Greta. Blackie and Greta were walking a circle, nose to tail the whole time, sniffing.

Cindy will never, as long as she lives, forgive Bruce for what he did that day. Cindy was in the trailer watching TV. It was hot. Bruce thought Cindy should be enjoying nature *outside* like him. After all, that's what he'd signed his life away to acquire.

Suddenly Bruce had flung open the trailer door for Bernice who was looking in through her blue frame glasses, her bleached blond hair rolled up in pink plastic curlers, sniffing. "Hi there, I'm Bernice from down the hill," she sniffed, eyes wide as Cindy lay on the sofa, naked as a jay bird.

The report of the "hippies-on-the-hill" was no doubt on that grapevine within minutes. For years Bruce and Cindy were the "hippies-on-the-hill." They'd overhear people who didn't know them give directions like this: "You go down south on Meek Road. There's the Spurr place on the right, a gray sided house." Then, they'd say (like Cindy and Bruce were a landmark), "Well, keep onna goin' past them hippie's-on-the-hill . . . "

"**I need you to write down my life's story!**" Jimmy's seventeen-year-old mouth with the dark fuzz above the upper lip blurts out as he stands facing Cindy squarely.

Without skipping a beat, Cindy answers, dryly, "Sorry! I don't do biographies." She would like to slam the door in his zitty face but that flirts with violence. Instead, she secretly revels in her comment and wishes that just once in her life someone were around who would appreciate the humor of a moment like this.

Snorting back some snot and picking at a pimple with a dirty fingernail, Jimmy looks seriously pitiful. Cindy thinks, dispassionately, that a writer would call the boy— crestfallen.

"I'm not really a writer," Cindy says softening a little. "I'm taking a class—just beginning. I've never had anything published, not one thing, but then, I've never tried." Jimmy doesn't look very satisfied. "I don't know if I have talent. I am *not* a writer—just a student—a student writer." Cindy's hands are fluttering all over the place as she confesses. Jimmy stands there—slump shouldered, swaying slightly like a feeble old man about to die. It's amazing how disappointment can seemingly age a person in seconds, Cindy thinks.

She can see that he's not satisfied. "When I write, it's about my *own* life," she continues, wondering why she is telling him that or anything for that matter? "That's what beginning writers are supposed to do—write about themselves—not somebody else." Her hands flutter back to resting perches on her hips. Finally she stops talking, relieved that she, a middle-aged woman, has quit defending herself—to of all people this kid with hormone troubles popping out his pores. [A middle-aged woman with hormone troubles vs. a teen with hormone troubles.]

"You'll have no problem gettin' this story published," Jimmy offers enthusiastically. 'Cause—it's bad!" Cindy's cool enough to know bad means good. "And since I'm *not no good with words*, I want you to write it down for me."

The cold air is still rushing past Cindy. Jimmy's trying to figure out a way to weasel his way into the house—same as Buster in the kennel behind him.

Cindy mocks Jimmy in her head:

> Oh, thank-you, kid! Thank-you for your *publishable* story. The tragic story of the farm kid and Suzy-Q who don't notice him no matter how many times he peels-out on the school's blacktop despite the suspension warnin' hangin' over his head and on top of that *boo hoo,* he's gonna flunk PE and it ain't his fault. Yummy—the Pulitzer!

"Can I use your bathroom?" Jimmy says rocking up and down ever-so-slightly on his toes, pushing an alarm inside Cindy. She had faced this rocking technique a lot when she substitute taught for extra money last winter. It was hard to tell a bluff and Cindy is vulnerable to this question since she peed her pants three times in first grade—twice because the teacher didn't believe she had to go.

"Well, can I use your bathroom?" Jimmy asks, rocking up and down more.

"Okay! Okay!" Cindy says as she sweeps him into the darkened house, flips the light switch and pulls the door shut behind him. He gets a few steps in when Cindy yells, "FREEZE!" Jimmy stops dead in his tracks, with his weight on one foot, clutching his K-Mart bag close to his chest. Cindy points down to the floor and says, "Don't you look where you're going? You almost stepped on that spider!"

Jimmy looks down to see a black spider scurry across the hardwood floor and under a chair.

"All clear," Cindy announces. "The bathroom is down that hall and on the left." She gestures the way for Jimmy as she thinks, I'll kill you, kid, if you dribble on my linoleum.

Two

Jimmy walks out of the bathroom. He sees Cindy sitting at the table with her eyes closed. Jimmy stands quietly and looks around. Man, this is a weird house, he thinks. The house is filled with stuff Jimmy's never seen on a wall in any house or anywhere.

On the wall behind the table is a large painting of a buxom nude woman with a big hat on her head, laying across the yellow do-not-pass line, in the center of an asphalt road. Draped around her neck like a fur collar is a fat, little dog body with Marilyn Monroe's face. Both of them look dead—especially because of the tire tread running across the woman's body, from her hip to her opposite breast. At the bottom of the painting floating across the road are the words: broad kill.

On the wall behind Jimmy's kitchen table at home is a painting of the Lord's Supper that his ma did from a kit she got from Big Ma one Christmas. Jimmy likes it even though Judas's face and the Doubting Thomas's hands didn't get completely painted. There's a number "13" printed on them in a couple of places. "They didn't give me enough of number thirteen," his ma complained. But you have to look close to see the colorless spot with the number on it.

Jimmy squints to read the words on the body of a crudely made red and yellow snake that makes "s" curves across the wall near the table where Cindy sits. The words say: "Never

25

eat anything with a face! O.K.?" Jimmy wonders if that's dirty.

They have a wooden cross at Jimmy's house hanging by the stairs. It says, "Jesus aves." The "S" fell off and got lost. Jimmy told his ma once that she should throw it out. But, his ma explained it's all they have of Jimmy's Dad's ma. It was one of the few small things she forgot to take when she ran off and left behind the big things—like her three kids.

Jimmy's ma would die if she saw that snake hanging in somebody's house. Jimmy wonders if it's satanic. It's one of those things that most people would see somewhere and wonder what would *anyone* do with such a thing? Jimmy thinks it's so weird that he kind of likes it, especially if it's what he thinks it might be—dirty or satanic.

"What are you doing?" Cindy urgently inquires as she springs out of her chair.

"Just lookin' at things," a startled Jimmy says.

"Did you put the lid down?" Cindy sounds like a parent, of all things—something she chose not to be " . . . because we've got a cat around here and she expects the lid to be down when she jumps on the toilet."

Jimmy says, "Yeah." But, Cindy doesn't trust him and goes to check.

When she comes back, Jimmy says, "See, I told ya."

Cindy responds with an irritated, "Come over here and sit down," as she motions toward the table with six candles in the middle of it, six smoking candles that once upon a time, long ago in a faraway place where strangers dwelled—heightened romance but now heighten sorrow.

She's been sittin' here in the dark with spiders crawling around, Jimmy thinks, burnin' candles, with weird stuff on the walls, watchin' tragedies on *Rescue 911.* He's always wanted to know one of those kind of people. He thinks it's pretty cool to be sitting in the house of a devil worshiper. He always heard they're hard to spot. You could walk right by them on the street and not know that they sacrificed a baby the night before and drank the blood. Jimmy wonders what Mrs. Mead has in her refrigerator.

When Cindy hears the chair creak and groan as Jimmy's rear hits it, Cindy wonders why it is that teenage boys can't sit down all nice-like? This kid is big like her older brother was as a teenager. For a period of about three years, her brother, Butch was always tripping on nothing. Overnight he sprouted great big feet, grew to be six-foot-three and smelled bad. Cindy remembers that after being her only companion all of her life (because they lived in the country and there were no other kids their age or any age within a mile) Butch all of a sudden wouldn't play with her any more, but kept right on punching her and wrenching her arm behind her back until she cried or said "Uncle" as many times as he decreed.

Well, here he is at Mrs. Mead's table. Jimmy is nervous. He's about to give what's in his K-mart bag to Cindy Mead. He doesn't want anything in the way of money for giving it to her. All Jimmy needs is to unburden himself.

Jimmy starts to cry a little. Oh, God, Cindy thinks, taken by surprise, the galoot is losing it. If he isn't who he is, Cindy might run to get a Kleenex, put it under his nostrils and say, "There, there, Jimmy—blow!" But he is who he is and she is who she is and so she sticks the knife in—it has to be done. *"You sure look an awful lot like one of those Trueberry boys down the road."* She thinks about twisting it by saying *HA! HA! GOTCHA!*

Cindy is referring to the second time Jimmy threw something at her when he showed up at her house last year and told her his name was Dave Chrysler. "Dave," he had said after looking at his beagle whom she already knew was named Dave. "Chrysler," he had said after searching for a few seconds and then eyeing his cousin's New Yorker. "My name is Dave Chrysler," the shit had announced looking straight into Cindy's eyes. It's one of those things that is permanently logged into Cindy's brain—and so this time, she twists the knife—a little.

"Maybe you're *related* to the Trueberry's, Dave." She pauses and adds, sarcastically, "Mr. Dave Chrysler."

Jimmy squirms in his chair. "I'm real sorry about that," he says, sniffing. "I didn't want you callin' my house. How's Dave and Slime?" he asks in a more chipper tone than before. Cindy wants to slug him.

The day that she met Jimmy face-to-face, down there in the driveway, a short, scrawny teenager was busy trying to stuff into the ripped up back seat of a rusty car, a beagle dog who didn't want to go and had no collar to use as a handle. The kid had caught the dog midair several times trying to jump out of the car. "Oh, no you don't, Dave!" he had said as he pitched the dog back in until finally he had slammed the door with the beagle inside howling up a storm.

"I think you shut Dave in the door!" Cindy had yelled, trying to get the door open.

"Ah, he's all right. He's just a big baby!" scrawny had said as Cindy had looked in the window to see for herself. He wasn't "all right." He was unhappy, but he wasn't shut in the door, either.

"Slime! Slime!" a voice on the other side of the house had hollered like he was calling someone.

Cindy had looked at "Scrawny" standing beside her in a jeans jacket with black skulls marching across the back with the words "Death Devils Rock On" written in a pretty cursive underneath. Then, she took a shot at him, "You're being paged, Slime."

The kid had answered in that uppity teenage tone, "Chill out!" Cindy knew he wanted to add, "bitch", but he had pointed to the east side of the house instead where there's a steep drop-off made by a glacier and had said, "Slime down over that hill."

As Cindy had headed that way she'd heard a commotion in the weeds and someone saying "Drop it, Slime, don't do it, drop it, yer gonna be sorry, drop it, Slime, Slime, drop it!"

Cindy was terrified that one of her old cats was in the mouth of a dog that those boys had brought here and turned loose. Cindy was frozen in place, whimpering, when behind her, "Scrawny" hawked up a wad of phlegm and spit it at the ground right beside Cindy's foot. Just as she looked down to see exactly how close that snot's snot had come to her shoe, something had burst from out of the weeds and into Cindy's peripheral vision.

Before she could react a muscular brown dog with a grin had bounced past her. He was humped up in the middle and bucking like those rodeo bronco steers with their genitals cinched tight with a leather strap. (Cindy once read that that's what makes them buck.) The creature was carrying one of those awful farm caps. The males around here wear them until they become filthy polyester and plastic rags perched on top of their heads like crowns on red neck royalty.

Right behind the dog came a big, muscular, stringy-haired kid. "Slime, you bitch, gimme that cap," he had yelled as they headed toward the sheds at the west edge of the property, plowing through Cindy's dead mums. Fatso and

Domino who'd been slinking around all morning, hissing, growling, and spraying things in the other's wake called a truce and *for once* in agreement had hustled themselves under a shed—together.

The dog had acted like it had springs on its feet as it bounced around four-and-a-half feet ahead of the kid. Cindy had hoped it had stuck a fang in that foul cap. She's been in the Crossroads Cafe where all of the men and boys are wearing those unsanitary things right through their meal.

Finally when Slime, who happened to be a female, had given up the cap, Jimmy had got her in the car after a big struggle. The dog had shaken her head and slimed the interior. Strings of saliva stuck to the windows. The big, gawky kid had turned to Cindy and had said, "Travis and me, we heard you take dogs in."

"No, I do not," Cindy had said firmly to the boy. "I take in dogs that *I* find. I do not take other people's dogs." Both dogs were barking inside the car, distracting Cindy. "I *do not* take animals from people," Cindy had spoken firmly. She never uses a contraction when she wants to sound firm. She had said it again, "I *do not* take in animals." Inside she was Jell-o. She didn't want to have to deal with two more dogs. It wasn't a good time. Cindy was too shaky right then. She'd driven six boney, old pets to the vets in the past year-and-a-half to have them put to death. Her precious dog, Marilyn, had disappeared four weeks before. And something was wrong with Cindy—her marriage, her life. Something was wrong.

"Are they your dogs?" she had asked. Jimmy had told her that his parents were dead and he was living with his grandfather and both of the dogs were strays that he'd been feeding. Jimmy had said, "My granpap give me until tonight to get rid of 'em. He told me at breakfast that he was goin' to shoot 'em after supper if they was still there."

30

Cindy had looked in the car at the beagle that was bigger than a regular beagle with longer legs. "I know that dog," she'd said remembering a dog that looked like that one chained to a dog house back in the field behind the Trueberry's. She'd been feeling sorry for that dog for a couple of years. "I think he belongs down the road at that run-down, white farmhouse, that kind of trashy looking place," she said waving in that direction. She had no idea she was talking to a Trueberry. "And that one," she'd said pointing to the obviously young, purebred of some kind, "someone's probably looking for that one. People don't dump purebreds."

"All I know," the kid said that day, "is if I come back with these dogs, *they're dead* and I'm supposed to be home at two. I tried dumpin' 'em out but my cousin's car wouldn't accelerate fast enough and I couldn't get away from 'em." There went Cindy's theory about purebred dumping. "Me and my cousin, we've been drivin' around all mornin' tryin' to figure out what to do and then my other cousin, Melinda, who rode with us for a while said we oughta take 'em to you— cause she heard you take dogs in."

"I-do-not-take-in-dogs," Cindy had repeated again, slowly, firmly. The kid's head had fallen forward, pitifully, onto his chest as the two dogs inside the car continued to bark at her and wag their tails furiously. Cindy had looked at them and heard the boy's words, "they're dead."

"Take them up and put them in the kennel," she had finally said, knowing all along she would. You'd have thought she'd said, "You boys have won a red Corvette," the way they both acted. One of them may have even whooped but Cindy couldn't tell through all of the commotion of getting those two dogs up to the kennel. When the gate swung shut, Cindy had turned to the big galoot and said, "What's your name?" To which he'd replied, "My name is Dave . . . *Dave Chrysler.*"

After they left that day, Cindy started thinking, She decided that the big kid looked like a kid she's seen at the Trueberry's house as she's gone by there over the years. Cindy had never met a Trueberry but she used to walk for exercise with someone who lives down that way. Debby had her picture window shot out by a Trueberry boy who was threatening to kill her asthmatic son who was perched in a tree in his own yard and afraid to move. That's who Cindy called to get the *real* story on the dogs and "Mr. Dave Chrysler."

This afternoon, Cindy looks straight into Jimmy's eyes and says, again "What's your name?" Jimmy looks straight back like he did that day and says, "Jimmy Trueberry—only I don't want you to use that when you write the story. My dad would pull the trigger on us all, if he knowed the truth like I do. He'll kill us just like he was going to kill Dave and Slime." *He'll kill us*—Cindy's heart flips at any suggestion of violence.

"This is it," Jimmy announces as he reaches for the K-mart sack in front of him, "My life's story." He holds the bag over the table and turns it upside-down. Little scraps of paper flutter out like big snowflakes, which excites Merryweather, the old yellow cat who hunts for things in motion. Merryweather does a fast wobble over to the table. She's nineteen and she'll soon be out in the pet graveyard squeezed in next to Nicky and Toot, Chester and Fatso and Domino and all of the others. If Merryweather dies in winter, she'll spend some time in the Styrofoam cooler in the shed like her mother, Black Magda who was put to sleep last winter and couldn't be planted until May because of the late spring.

Even at nineteen, Merry's a food monger, probably from a long line of scrappy, country cats. She and her mother proved every day of their lives in true Darwinian fashion that *they are the fittest*—fitter than Cindy—fitter than Bruce—fitter than any other cat or any dog. Cindy wouldn't want to meet the being that could get a piece of food away from a *Nagger*, the surname they gave those cats because of their relentless meowing and aggression in the presence of food.

Merry tries to use Jimmy's lap as a midway launch for the table top but she gets stuck . . . on his leg . . . and dangles by her front claws. Old cat claws don't retract well. They stick out most of the time, snagging things and getting caught. Cindy knows it's time to clip when she finds Merry stuck here or there—the bedspread, the carpet, Bruce's chair, time to wrap Merry tightly in a towel, including her head because it has "the mouth"—leaving out one paw at a time—time to clip nails and be clipped by a foul tempered old bat-of-a-cat who can scissor her way through anything.

Merry is stuck to Jimmy's leg. Jimmy raises his open hand. By god, Cindy believes he is going to strike Merry. Jimmy catches Cindy's eyes focused intensely on him. She looks poised to lunge. He knows Cindy from talk around the area. When Jimmy remembers he wants Cindy to write his story, his raised hand decides to scratch his head instead. He knew her first as that "hippie-on-the-hill" and then, as that "loony animal lady."

Good boy, Cindy thinks. He must know I'm the *loco humanitarian.*

Jimmy thinks, maybe she ain't a Satanist. Maybe she's a witch. Witches are into cats.

Cindy thinks about thumping Jimmy in the head when she remembers how she got two dogs dumped on her by a bald-faced liar but her finger tips thump the table instead. His whole story was a lie. She took this kid's very own dogs, found a good home for the one. She gave her home to the other one that nobody wanted—not even her. She'd be damned if she'd give the beagle to one of those hunters who were the only ones to respond to the classified ad.

33

Cindy hopes that Merryweather Nagger has shredded Jimmy's leg or at least made it bleed a little. Cindy had enough to deal with in her life at that time without having some lying kid make her responsible for his dogs. Jimmy moans as he reaches for Merry and says, "Here kitty, let me help ya." Then he gently lifts her up until her claws let go. He places her on his lap and flashes a phony grin at Cindy as he pets Merry. Merryweather begins to purr audibly.

Bruce and Cindy only started to hear her purr several months ago. Before that, the only way you could tell if she was purring was to feel the vibration on her sides—if you could catch her and then through some miracle get her into a good mood. Bruce and Cindy used to herd her around the house like she was a wounded bull in a bullfight. "You go over there with the broom," Cindy would instruct Bruce. "If she comes out from behind the TV when I stomp back here, you steer her out that open door." Merry's always assumed every living thing was out to kill her—even Bruce and Cindy— that's been her delusion. She never sat on a lap or purred until a few months ago. Now if she's not hunting for food, she's hunting for a lap. "It's a miracle," Cindy commented to Bruce on Merry's old age eleventh-hour conversion. "Praise the lord!" she shouted. "That's what I plan to do. Repent at the last minute," she'd added.

The funny thing (funny peculiar, not funny ha, ha) is that Merryweather and her sisters Flora and empty-in-the-attic Fauna were almost born in Cindy's lap in the trailer. Cindy was macraméing a necklace, singing to a song on Bruce's station. *"I beg your pardon, I never promised you a rose garden."* Cindy thought Black Magda up and peed on her bell bottoms because they didn't even know Black Magda was pregnant when her water broke. She wasn't really their cat. She was not a Nagger then. She was Mike Spurr's little sister's cat, "Nigger."

Merryweather never had to fight one day for food. It was always there, dry food in her own bowl along with a daily serving of canned stuff—tuna delight, mixed grill, chicken livers and chopped cow tongues—you name it. The Naggers were big time hunters who functioned all their lives as though they never knew where the next meal was coming from—same as Bruce's mom and her kids—after his dad's breakdown and the divorce.

Cindy has never had a pet that wasn't difficult. The good ones go to other homes through ads in the paper and careful screening. Cindy always issues a guaranteed return policy. She couldn't live with knowing that an animal who'd passed through her house ended up at the pound or was dumped again.

The complete undesirables were never advertised. No point. They stayed right here. Cindy catered to their peculiarities and ailments until the day they died. There was Chester from *Gunsmoke* who came to them with a stiff leg that had to be amputated. Chester hopped around on three legs for ten years. Betty-the-cat's pupils were permanently dilated from a head wound—BB's. She had to squint in bright light and she fell off things all of the time. She fell off the woodpile and broke her tail. It had to be amputated. For years Cindy was running back and forth to the vets to have an animal fixed up or killed when it couldn't be fixed up.

As of last month, the Mead household is down to Merryweather and Buster after a high at one time in those twenty years of three permanent dogs and twelve permanent cat residents. Ten years ago she started looking away when she spotted an animal in need of a rescue. She never consciously acknowledged that she began looking away. De Nile. It would be too difficult to know what she was doing and why.

Merryweather Nagger is sitting contentedly, kneading on Jimmy's leg. He's being brave. Cindy reaches over to pick up one of the bigger scraps of paper which has been torn out of a spiral notebook and then torn in half. "I wrote it down as it come to me," Jimmy says. "One part of the story is on a napkin from the cafeteria 'cause that's where I remembered somethin'—durin' lunch. I'll have to tell the story to you so you'll know how to put these pieces of paper together."

She reads the scratchings on the paper:

> *I was a little guy when Charlie Yates he held me in his arms. Man, was he big. His arms was big. His neck was big. He patted my back and said something like You are all right son.* **Yor Daddy will keep you safe.** *Witch I never forgot and even then thoght was kind of strange. After, all, he was talking to a kid who just seen his Daddy run over and kill his little brother."*

Cindy is afraid to take her eyes off the paper. She's afraid to look at Jimmy. Cindy's overcome with a craving for anything sweet and brown. She rushes to the refrigerator, even though she knows there's nothing sweet in there except a squeeze bottle of chocolate syrup of which she takes a swig. Jimmy suspects that Cindy is squeezing sacrificial blood out of that bottle.

Merryweather leaps off Jimmy's lap and practically goes splat as her legs splay out beneath her. She picks herself up and clicks her claws across the hardwood floor to the refrigerator. Cindy's eyes are on the crud stuck to the metal shelf but she doesn't see crud or anything. She repeats to herself—his daddy *ran over his brother.* God!

Jimmy gets comfy as he pitches his cap into the nearby vinyl chair which is a mistake because the chair turns into a cat and dog hair magnet in the dry winter air of the wood-heated house. Jimmy takes off his jacket. He has on a black Eastern High T-shirt.

Cindy shuts the refrigerator door and goes back to sit at the table. Merry is on delay—stuck at the refrigerator, wondering where Cindy went. The refrigerator whir-rat-rats again.

Jimmy rocks back on two legs of the chair. Absolutely no substitute teacher allows that but Cindy doesn't say anything other than, "My husband will be home soon and I'd like to read these papers before I go any further." Cindy sounds so businesslike, even to herself. "Why don't you give me your telephone number and I'll call you about it."

"Mrs. Mead," Jimmy says with an earnest sincerity that surprises Cindy. He leans forward and says, "Seriously, my dad can't know about this, not my ma either. But, if I don't get this story outa me, I'm gonna go berserk. Please, Mrs. Mead, write my story down for me."

Cindy looks into the sorry brown eyes of a whipped pup and hears a calling to a rescue. "Okay, I'll write it and call me Cindy." Jimmy tips back again in his chair, thumps his thigh in rhythm and says, "Allllll Riiiiight!" Without missing a beat, he adds, "These are my conditions"—like he is the one with the bargaining power. "You can't use my real name and you got to make up a bunch of other stuff. I don't want nobody to recognize nobody."

"Is that all?" Cindy asks in a tone that suggests she's involved in espionage.

"No, I want my name to be Dack . . . Dack Dick."

Cindy tries to suppress a laugh when she says, "Dack Dick?"

"Yeah, Dack Dick!" Jimmy says firmly. He's irritated as he explains to Cindy that it's not any weirder than a lot of band names, and that's what he decided a long time ago would make a "bad" name for a band and since he's not never going to have a band because he can't play a thing he wants his name in this story to be Dack Dick which he already calls himself anyway when he talks to himself—although he doesn't tell Cindy that part. It's Dack Dick this and Dack Dick that! When he turns on the ignition in his car, Jimmy announces, "Dack Dick starts his engine" and imagines himself a driver in the Indy 500 or when he leaps off the hay loft into the pile of straw below, he hollers, "Dack Dick to the rescue!"

Dack Dick. Cindy rolls it around in her mind. Once Bruce and Cindy were at the little airport in town waiting for Bruce's mom's commuter flight from Chicago, the last leg from Kansas City. There were about twenty anxious teenage girls, waving their hands out the windows toward the runway. Cindy had asked one girl what was going on and she'd said, indignantly, "Lynyrd Skynyrd."

"Oh," Cindy had responded.

Bruce had leaned over and asked, "What's going on?"

Cindy had answered, "Lynyrd Skynyrd."

"What?" Bruce had questioned.

Cindy had said again, pronouncing it slowly and clearly, "Len-erd Skin-erd."

Bruce had said, "Oh."

Cindy found out the next day from the *Citizen-Times* that Lynyrd Skynyrd is a rock band that had played the Reed County Fair and Petunia Festival. Lynyrd Skynyrd! Dack Dick! Cindy understood—sort of. It doesn't really matter to Cindy anyway. She plans to rough out this story, hand it to Dack Dick, and be on with her life. She has no idea why she's willing to do that much, other than she's a sucker for a being, human or non human in distress. Bruce will be all pissed off about the whole thing. He says she doesn't spend enough time with him. She's always "fiddling around with something useless." Now, she'll be writing a story for no good reason for a no good kid.

Cindy won't tell him. She'll do it without his knowing. She'll sneak-write like she sneak-eats. "You've got to go, Jimmy," Cindy says remembering that Bruce will be home any minute. Cindy stands up. Jimmy thumps the chair back down on four legs. He reaches for his cap and sticks it on his head in one swoop. It has yellow cat hair stuck to the navy-colored polyester part on the front that has the Dekalb embroidery of an ear of corn with wings on it.

Jimmy stops to look at a framed photograph on a round table beside a chair in the living room. It's in a pewter frame that looks like the outside of a dog house complete with shingles and a raised bone at the door.

Inside the opening of the doghouse, Cindy is smiling, crouching down in snow, hugging her Marilyn who looks to Cindy like a Marilyn Monroe dog—blonde hair, black eye liner and a slightly-plump-by-today's-standards, rounded body. . . and, that Marilyn had a flirty way—and a black beard, but Cindy doesn't count that. Nobody including the vet had ever seen a dog that even came close to looking like Marilyn.

Cindy thought Bruce was going to have a fit when he came home to find Marilyn in the kennel that day, but he went right to her and started petting and said, "You're cute!" And when Cindy had told him that someone down the road had seen her pitched out the window of a car that sped off as the dog stood there in the ditch, frozen in place, Bruce had petted harder. Cindy knew he'd love the dog more because of that story which was the truth—but he'd not want to admit it—"too twinkie." He guarded his sympathies. And, he didn't want anyone to think he was "attached" to anyone or anything—except maybe that Harley that he rarely rides—mostly looks at.

Bruce was a German Shepherd man but since the first one he'd bought and then had to leave with his brother, Bob, when he moved to Michigan and into that trailer court, he'd accepted whatever came their way although he is always acting like they were foisted on him by Cindy. He's the one who turned around at the next exit and raced back up Interstate 69 that Christmas eve to save Nicholas who'd been cutting back and forth across all four lanes, causing people to brake and swerve. Cindy was too afraid to suggest it—afraid she'd lose more of her feelings for Bruce. Since she's the one who coaxed Nick into the car, everyone on both sides of the family thinks she's responsible for the house full of pets that Bruce always complained about to his mom, to her mom, to anyone within earshot.

Cindy picks up the frame. "Jimmy, this is Marilyn," she says to Jimmy, like an introduction.

Cindy remembers how Marilyn was "adopted out" twice and brought back twice. The second couple had taken her to be a companion in an adult foster care home where the house parents tried to make Marilyn sleep on a rug on the floor beside their bed when Marilyn knew the real soft bed was right there above her head, calling "yoo-hoo." "It was up, down, up, down, all night long," the woman had said when she brought her back. "We wanted a smart dog." Cindy had responded, "Wow, I'll bet she wanted a smart owner, too." The clever little reject stayed at Cindy's.

And then there was that Sunday. The Spurr's two hundred dollar Lab—eight months old, lovable but dumber than shit, had come up to the Mead's yard and he and Marilyn had romped into the woods together. Cindy remembers wandering acres of woods all by herself, calling both of their names, sobbing and for once not caring who saw her cry. She'd put an ad in the paper for both dogs. She'd put out a reward poster. She'd lost ten pounds without even trying. Neither dog was ever seen again and nothing, no collar or tag was ever found of either one.

Cindy remembers cursing Rita Spurr from her yard. In an uncontrollable fit one day the next week, Cindy had run out into her yard, cupped her hands around her mouth, and had yelled down over the hill, "Why the hell didn't you keep Rex in your own yard? Why the hell couldn't you work with me on this? Don't you fuckers know that dogs run in packs? Of course you know—there's always a pack of Spurrs down there." Then, she'd turned around with her nose in the air and went back into her house feeling better. The next day, August third (Cindy put it on her calendar), Rita had propped the huge speaker to their stereo system in the upstairs window that faces Cindy's house, turned the radio full blast to a country music station and had left the house until eleven o'clock that night.

"I love you!" Cindy professes to the photograph of her Marilyn Monroe look-alike as she kisses the glass. From the looks of it, the glass has been kissed a lot. "She had so much personality—and smart as a whip," she says to Jimmy who is standing beside her. When she glances at Jimmy, he seems frozen. She figures she's boring him or maybe spooking him—he looks spooked—but she says anyway, "I don't think I'll ever get over never seeing that little dog again." Cindy chokes on what she says next, "You know, never knowing what happened—never knowing. She was too young to die." Cindy catches herself. She shouldn't be talking like that to Jimmy, with his little brother and all. Cindy wonders if Jimmy's little brother died quickly? "If Marilyn is dead," she can't help but say, "I pray it was quick and painless. Was it quick and painless," Cindy hesitates as she looks at Jimmy, "with your little brother?"

"I gotta go!" Jimmy says as he shoves the plastic bag at her and lets himself out. The door at the bottom of the stairwell opens at the same time and Bruce hollers up in that harsh, sarcastic voice that makes Cindy want to punch him in the face, "There's an old wreck down here blocking the driveway and I can't get up the hill!"

By the time Bruce got back out there, Jimmy was gone and Cindy told Bruce that the kid was selling chocolates for the

Eastern High Band but she didn't order any. Bruce doesn't eat candy and Cindy doesn't either. Ha! You don't want candy, the prosecutor mocks her in her head all day, every day. You don't want to get fat. The defense offers that Cindy *doesn't* want to get fat, but she most surely *does* want chocolate candy and forcefully adds directly to the phantom jury—twenty-four hours a day!

"How was your day?" Cindy asks like she does every afternoon as she gives him an obligatory peck on the lips to maintain some semblance of normalcy.

"'Bout like always. Only one more day until the weekend," Bruce adds, as he unloads a grocery bag while Cindy contemplates Dack Dick's dad and his little son that he ran over.

Cindy goes out to get Buster to bring him into the house for the night. "Jimmy asked about you, Dave," she tells Buster who is jumping all over her, happy to be going inside the house where a half-a-can of dead cow awaits and the litter pan torments.

"Dave! Dave!" Cindy calls out, trying to see if he recognizes his old name. He keeps alternately jumping on her and on the gate.

Cindy sees smoke—white against a gray sky, poofing out the chimney in little spurts that look like they're trying to connect but never quite do before they become invisible. Bruce is down in the basement, poking through ashes stirring up some red hot coals smoldering under there— throwing kindling on and mumbling that Cindy about let the fire go out. Buster is jumping on her but Cindy stands there with no coat on watching the smoke, with the leash in her hand, wishing she didn't have to go back in there and feeling guilty about feeling that way.

Three

"I done it!" Jimmy says as Starr gets into his car in her black Spandex skirt and over the knee leather boots with the highest heels she could find.

"What did you do?" Starr asks flipping the visor mirror down so she can spread more iridescent magenta-rose across her pouty lips. She discovered they were *pouty* in an article in *Glamour* magazine. There were pictures and labels on all kinds of lips showing how to make them up to maximize the good ones and improve the not-so-good ones. Starr's lips are good. She believes they're more seductive now that she outlines them with a pencil that's a shade darker than the lipstick color, like they showed in the article. Next, she'll rat her bangs up a little higher—if she can get a comb in there—it's sprayed pretty stiff with Pow-Wow-WOWER Ultra Spritzer that Chastity told her about.

"I went to see the writer-lady yesterday," Jimmy says.

Starr gets out her comb, brush, pick and spritzer and goes to work. "And, what did she say?"

"She said she'll do it!"

"Greeeaaat!" Starr says, her voice trailing off as she becomes distracted. "Honk at Matt Riley!" she suddenly commands and Jimmy honks while Starr flutters her long, pink press-on fingernails and smiles coyly out the side window. She turns to Jimmy and barks another order, "Get outa here before the buses pull out!" Jimmy tries to gun it. The New Yorker doesn't gun. It slowly picks up speed.

Jimmy loves the sound of his muffler as he accelerates and heads down County Farm Road. Right now he's glad that Starr managed to get her parents to put off private school for another year and let her go to Eastern High. She's told Jimmy that time is running out and that makes Jimmy feel fatalistic. Starr has explained "fatalism" to Jimmy even though she doesn't believe in it. "I believe you control your destiny," she has told Jimmy.

Starr's parents have for years been telling her, "We trust you to make good decisions." Joan, Starr's mother, learned about that in a positive parenting class when Starr was two. Lately Joan's deeply held liberal philosophy is beginning to fall apart. College "looms" over Joan's head not Starr's. Privately—Starr has no intention of going to college.

Once, when Starr was mad at her mother, she overheard her parents discussing school. Joan had made her first effort at parental-imposed discipline by suggesting earlier that day that she might put a time limit on how much Starr could talk on the phone each week. When Starr overheard the conversation about school, her parents were unaware that she was crawling below them, under the deck, to see if she could unplug or snip a wire to her mother's deck extension phone as a response to such a stupid comment about controlling Starr's phone habits.

While under there she'd heard her mother bitchily say, she believes this school problem they're finally having to face, could have been avoided ten years ago, when they built the house. Her mother told Starr's dad, Steve, he should have known that what was to become their thirty acres of woods south of the country club was over the Reedville line putting it into the Eastern District. "After all," she'd said, "he was the one who handled it with that real estate agent, Suzette something." Joan had expressed, with a lament in her voice, that they should have built where she wanted to, at Melody Lake, where the lots are large and the neighbors more appealing. And, even though one couldn't call the school system in Reedville fantastic, it's superior to Reedville.

Steve, who had gone to a small rural school himself, had responded, "Starr's happy. She's doing very well, academically." Then, he'd sounded like he was trying to use her language to appease her. "Serendipity! It was meant to be," he'd said, shrugging his shoulders as if to say "what more can I say." Starr had observed through the deck cracks that her father mumbled off to soak in the hot tub. Joan's arms were outstretched as if lost in question while she muttered, "What in the world did he mean by *that?*"

Starr continues to go to Eastern. According to letters Starr found next to Joan's computer, Joan has explored the idea of paying tuition to Reedville. The Reedville school board had expressed sympathy to Joan's worry that Starr would not be developing good computer skills because the Eastern District voters have not passed a millage in four years, and there is no money for more computers—let alone better ones. Still, a transfer is out of their hands. Eastern will not let a student transfer to another district because of the money they get from the state for each student.

Joan worries about computers. In her appeal to the board, she'd faxed, "As an educator, myself, I know that in this day and age, young people must be computer literate to succeed." Essentially, the Reedville School Board faxed back: "True, and too bad for you!"

Even though Starr is a straight "A" student and she's taking the college prep track, Starr is not going to college. She hasn't told Joan and Steve yet. They're going to die! She knows it. Whose life is it anyway? Starr plans to go to Acme Academy of Beauty in Lansing like Chastity, her former baby-sitter whom Starr credited in an English essay as having been the greatest influence on her life. Chas is too cool. She's the one who processes Starr's hair in the piggyback, spiral roll with the 2 K 1 solution while she tells Starr about Cedar Woods Apartments and all the cute guys that she meets at the pool.

Starr's a freshman. Jimmy's a Sophomore who should be a Junior. They held him back in first grade. His dad had objected. Mr. Joseph, the principal, had told Eugene that Jimmy needed another year to mature. Eugene had declared to Mr. Joseph, "My kid don't need no coddlin'." But Eugene had no clout at the school. Jimmy thinks he'll quit like his brother. He's old enough now. If he quits he'll probably never see his Starr again. So he's hanging in there until they take Starr away.

It's Thursday and Starr isn't exactly looking forward to a weekend at home with *them*. She's had a rough week with three exams, making Starr ready to party. "Jimmy," Starr says, "let's get some brew and drive out to the lake! I need to relax!"

"Where we gonna get it?" Jimmy asks, knowing exactly where.

"Drive by my house."

Starr knows her mother is at the community college. She teaches Theater Lighting until six tonight and her dad—who knows when he'll be home. He's a workaholic who owns a color printing business that prints slick color brochures for *concerns* all over the state. Before he dies, he plans to be a millionaire—not including what Joan brought to the marriage. More to the point, he plans to be a millionaire before his old man dies. But with the chest pains Steve's been loudly announcing lately, it's hard to tell who's going to get the last word on anything.

Starr gets a four-pack of tropical-something wine coolers from the refrigerator behind the bar downstairs in the entertainment room. She takes the phone in her room off the hook so if her mom calls she'll get a busy signal. Starr can say later that she was helping a friend with math and then must not have gotten her phone back on the hook. She has to add that last part because she has call-waiting. Joan will accept that. Starr doesn't have to work too hard to fool her mother. To Starr, Joan always seems distracted or distraught by something other than what's going on at the moment.

Jimmy drives to Green Lake and pulls down one of the lanes that goes to an empty piece of property on the lake. It's always a challenge to get the New Yorker in and out of there. Starr and Jimmy like to live dangerously. The owner of the land lives in Toledo and only comes to camp on weekends during the summer. This is Starr and Jimmy's private place all year except for those two months of weekends.

Jimmy faces his Chrysler toward the lake. It's starting to snow. "It's so pretty here," Starr says, feeling more relaxed already. Jimmy wants to put his arm around Starr but instead he says, "I'm gonna cut school tomorrow and go over to the writer's house and tell her the whole story."

"I thought you already did."

"No, I just got 'er to agree to write it."

"Oh," Starr says laying her head back and letting her knees fall apart.

Jimmy eyes the knees, takes a big swig of cooler, drums with his fingertips onto his thighs, and says, "Kinda weird, that lady."

"Weird, how?"

"She's different from your ma or my ma. Your ma's a bitch. My ma's a whore." Jimmy decides not to tell Starr yet about Cindy Mead being a witch or a Satan worshiper.

"Do you think this will be a symbiotic relationship?" Starr asks. "I mean, do you think you'll be compatible? That'll be real important if she's going to write your life story."

Symbiotic! Jimmy loves that shit when Starr uses big words— even if it makes him feel dumb. In her own way, he knows that Starr loves him. They can really talk. Maybe someday they can do what Jimmy thinks about a lot. Jimmy's not given up on that, yet. Nobody knows Jimmy better than Starr and Starr says that nobody knows her better than Jimmy. It has been that way since the fourth grade when Starr discovered Jimmy crying behind the milk machine in the cafeteria. He's belonged to her ever since. She defends him when those snobs make fun of him. That's why he was behind the milk machine. Trent Howard had told him that his mother had said Jimmy Trueberry looks like a ragamuffin!

"Ragamuffin! Ragamuffin!" Trent had gotten everybody else going.

Starr actually talks to him in the halls. She doesn't care who's looking. Starr's got a heart of gold. That's for sure, Jimmy thinks. She had hugged Jimmy back there in the cobwebs behind that machine and said, "There! There!" like he was her great big doll. The last hug Jimmy can remember before that was the one from Charlie Yates the day Jimmy's little brother was killed. Jimmy's family doesn't hug. Starr's parents hug her all the time and they're always saying, *I love you*—all the time, out of the blue, for no reason at all. Starr thinks it's a bit much. In fact, she'd put her foot down last year demanding they stop with the "love stuff". Jimmy still thinks it sounds kind of nice. Although he'd probably heave if one of his parents said it to him.

Starr's parents don't like the way she dresses. She knows it. She also knows they can't make her change her style. After all—Joan *trusts* her. Steve is so unsure of what he should be doing as a parent that he's never taken much of a stand on anything to do with Starr. Starr has them figured out.

Starr's seen some pretty ridiculous photos of her mother with long, flat, mousy-brown hair parted in the middle. She was wearing jeans with the bottoms of each leg bigger around than the waistband, no makeup, standing on some thick soled sandals, looking anemic. Starr has a tan year-round from the Hawaiian Tanner in Reedville. "Bogus, Joan," Starr says to her mother whenever she looks through the photograph album. Steve has a crew cut in some of his undergraduate pictures and an ROTC uniform. He's a little older than Joan. They met when Steve was in college—using the GI bill after Vietnam. Joan was working on her doctorate, which she never finished, choosing instead to marry Steve and move to of all places, *Reedville*. She tells everyone, "I never intended to have a daughter of mine grow up in Reed County, Michigan." Such comments don't exactly endear her to the community boosters, most of whom have lived here all of their lives.

Steve had come back from Vietnam changed—in opposition. He and Joan both had protested the war together, and in six months had married in a park under a tamarack tree where Joan had felt "good vibes." Her parents were horrified. They'd always expected a big church wedding when Joan married and a reception at the country club in Grand Rapids. Joan had grown up expecting that, too. But, times were different. Her mother still laments that Joan would have made such a beautiful bride, never conceding that the barefoot woman/child with the white Daisies in her hair and one painted on her cheek *was* a bride.

In truth, Joan does regret the whole thing. She's looking forward to planning a big production for Starr's wedding. Joan went crazy for a while in her youth. She'd entered college with a lacquered, lemon-lightened helmet on her head, false eyelashes and a wardrobe of Villager matching skirts and sweaters. She had left as a dishwater blonde, no makeup, straight hair to her waist, wearing ankle-length skirts she had made herself from Indian bedspreads and see-through, gauze blouses with no bra.

Now twenty-some years later, Starr sees that Joan and Steve have separate lives, though no one really acknowledges that. There's no love there—at least not the kind Starr believes will be in her marriage. There's a lot of sniper fire back and forth. Steve cloaks his shots in sarcasm, and when Joan doesn't laugh he reminds her that sarcasm is a form of humor. "For Christ's sake! Lighten up!" he often whines.

Starr has everything a teen could want—a room of her own (easy since she's an only child in a four bedroom house) authorization to use Joan's charge card at Jacobson's, her own phone and phone line, a great hair designer who's on the same wavelength, and when she's sixteen, Starr's sure she'll get a car without begging. It probably won't be brand new but, it *will* be sexy *and* black. Starr guarantees that! Her father promised.

What she doesn't have and wants is Matt Riley. Right now Matt has Heather Williams. Starr is patient though, because she knows that Heather is shallow and too Catholic. Matt will get tired of her and look for more excitement. Starr feels she's exciting or could be if she had the chance.

She's learned a lot from *Days of Our Lives* which she chooses to watch on tape after her parents think she's asleep. No need to bring them in on her taste in television. She's not about to watch public TV like Joan, or listen to classical music. Steve's all the time mimicking the voices of the men who narrate shows on PBS about the brain or China or the Constitution. Starr loves it when Steve makes fun of Joan. Once he had put on that resonate TV announcer's voice and did a blow by blow of Joan as she made a salad. He'd made it sound like rare and delicate surgery. *"The skillful hands of well-trained culinary surgeon, Joan Gillette make an incision on each end of the carrot, successfully amputating the roots and the top."*

Joan didn't think it was funny, because any minute she'd been expecting a Dean from the college and his wife, and she needed some help—not commentary from a "loaded jerk who was already embarrassing her."

Joan and Steve have never met nor heard about Jimmy. He's Starr's private friend like an imaginary playmate. They wouldn't like him. They wouldn't say it directly. Joan might say something like, "Jim, what do your parents do?" And when Jimmy answered, "My dad, he works on the line at Schultz Equipment and raises pigs on the side and my ma, she works at Harvest Bread Bakery mixin' dough", Joan would more-than-likely change the subject, ignoring Jimmy and say something like, "Starr, honey, the 'Y' is starting gymnastics classes soon. Should I sign you up?" Like she believed that Starr would actually consider messing up her hair.

Steve might say to Joan in a stage whisper in the kitchen, "I don't think he's going to be a *doctor*, Joan, or a *lawyer* or even a *college professor* or a **student** for that matter!" Then, he'd come out and slap Jimmy on the back and say something inane like, "Hey, Dude, want to go down to Red Dog's parking lot and siphon some gas?" Then, Steve would, as he often does, laugh with his clever self and follow his own beaten path down to his own bar in what he calls the "basement" and Joan calls the "entertainment" room. Like a ritual, he'd siphon some expensive alcohol into his system down there, attempt to read a stock market report, and pass out for the night with a purring Romeo rising and falling heavily on his chest. That's what he does every night.

Starr has them both figured out. Even though they're pretty good to her, Steve's a bastard and Joan's a basket case. "Your mother is having trouble coping," Steve had told Starr after one of Joan's "episodes" which Starr heard through her door.

"Coping with what?" Starr had queried.

"Life," Steve had answered but Starr knew it was him. Joan's having trouble coping with Steve and maybe Starr, too. But Starr loves them "unconditionally." She had told Jimmy that once when they were parked here, and then added, so he'd understand, "I love them despite their obnoxious behavior."

Jimmy scoots down in the seat, lays his head back and looks at the lake, past the camper trailer, through the pine trees. He'd rather have some beer—about a case. Starr and Jimmy don't have to talk all of the time—although she can really jaw when she gets going. Sometimes they do what they're doing right now—chill-out.

It's funny, Jimmy thinks, that he didn't even know his life was a puzzle until he found the last piece and put it in and now that he's fit all of the pieces together—his life is *one . . . fucking . . . mess* and he doesn't know what to do about it. At least he didn't until Starr had expressed in awe that his life turned out to be like something you'd read in a novel. Starr had explained that a novel is like a TV mini-series as a book. Jimmy understood that. He can clearly picture his life as a miniseries.

That's the point when Jimmy decided to find a writer to put his life in a book. That's when he'd asked his Aunt Rose if she knew of any writer of books around here and she'd said that she'd heard that the "hippie-on-the-hill" over on Meek Road is a writer. Of course, she had to ask why he wanted to know. Rose is snoopy. Jimmy had said, "Cause" and that ended it. The Trueberry men don't tell their females *nothin'*. It's different with Starr though. Jimmy eventually tells her everything.

Like his big brother Will, who left, Jimmy would be gone away somewhere if it wasn't for Starr. She's the reason he isn't "gone-for-good" as in "croaked"—like his little brother Terry. Jimmy had planned to "check out" on life *that fateful night* a little over a year ago. He was going to do *them* first and then kill himself. They were smashed together so tightly that he couldn't help but get them both in one shot—his ma and Charlie Yates in the old cabin at the back of their land where the two properties join.

Jimmy took off running to the house after he'd seen enough. He'd run up to his room and grabbed the Winchester Model 12 that his granpap left him. Jimmy was halfway back to the cabin with the gun when he saw those two shadowy figures come dancing on their paws across the west field in the moonlight. Coyotes, he'd thought. Old man Singer had been talking about a pack of coyotes that were roaming around killing his sheep. Nobody but Singer believed that there were coyotes around here. It wouldn't have mattered what or who they were. Jimmy had wanted to kill something. He'd aimed the shotgun, gritted his teeth and pulled. He was about sixty yards away when he "whacked 'em"—those fuckin' coyotes.

Right away there were some yelps, jumps and staggers. One of them ran on for quite a ways. Jimmy had watched it until it went down. Then he'd run up toward it but stopped about ten feet away. While it was still whining in the blackness he'd shot at it again and the whining stopped.

He'd backtracked to find the other one. It wasn't hard to spot since this one was light colored and glowed in the dark, looking like a small ghost laying there, on old brown stubs of corn stalks that Jimmy had made with the corn picker. The light colored thing was gurgling and every once in a while, some part of it would move. Jimmy wasn't sure what moved. Sometimes when it moved it would make a soft whine. "Goddamn coyotes," Jimmy had fumed. Mother fuckin' killers, he'd thought. Jimmy had run up to the thing and kicked it real hard. "Fuckin' killer," he'd said between his teeth. Boy, that kick made it yelp and so he'd kicked it again and again until all he could hear was the gurgling.

He'd whacked those coyotes. He'd whacked them real good. Dack Dick, the rock star, Indy racer and baddest hunter alive had whacked them. He'd turned around and kicked at the gurgles as hard as he could one more time as he'd spit, "And one to die on, fuckin' killer."

On that *fateful night*, as Starr always refers to it, Jimmy had talked to Starr on the phone at about ten-thirty. Right after their conversation Dack Dick went to the barn and jumped off the hay loft into a pile of straw. Starr gives him such burst of uneasy energy driving him to another place, one where he thinks best—granpap's old Allis-Chalmers that is still parked in the weeds right where it was the day he died. Jimmy was perched up on the seat, leaning over the steering wheel resting his head on his arms, when the back door, off the porch, had opened and here comes his ma.

Oh fuck, he'd thought, she must be lookin' for me. Both his parents go to bed early, like nine. At that time for about a month or so Jimmy had been getting restless, something in him was changing, and so, he'd taken to calling Starr late at night. Sometimes, Jimmy doesn't call Starr. Sometimes, he goes out to sit on the tractor or the front porch swing depending on the weather. His parents would assume Jimmy was upstairs in his bedroom. Will had been gone for about a month. Nobody would ever check upstairs now because Jimmy's not given them trouble like Will. His ma was always coming up the stairs to check on Will. Will is like his dad, Lizzie Jo would tell her sisters. He's got some meanness to him but Jimmy, he's sweet. "He's a good boy", she'd say. "He's different from the rest of the Trueberry tribe."

That night Jimmy had watched his ma walk across that yard in a straight line out the back door, past the barn and back the lane. Where the fuck is she going, Jimmy had wondered? She had on her nightgown under her jacket. She was holding it up to her knees with one hand while she clutched her jacket at the neck with the other. Her hair which comes to the middle of her back when it's not knotted up was flying behind her.

She'd almost disappeared when Jimmy decided to follow. He kept some good distance between them. It was while he was trailing his ma that he remembered the angel he'd seen several times when he was little after his brother was killed. A lot of nights he'd wake up and look out his upstairs window down to where he and Terry had played that awful morning. It was his fault that his brother died. His dad said so, right after it happened. He'd screamed to Jimmy, "You shoulda knowed better!" So Jimmy gazed out the window at night as he grew up and wondered how he could change what had happened. And sometimes, the angel in a long gown had swept across their yard—coming or going across the back yard. He'd seen her from his window upstairs but he never told anyone because he thought if his dad knew, he might try to shoot her.

Lizzie Jo was really trucking on down the lane that night into the woods with Jimmy stalking behind her. Jimmy had smelled wood smoke and then he'd seen a little glow of light. It was kind of spooky out that night with Halloween coming. What the fuck is ma doing back here? Jimmy wondered.

He'd heard her up ahead say loudly, "I'm here! It's me, Charlie!" Jimmy had stopped and watched from behind a brush pile. Charlie Yates had come out of his old hunting cabin in the woodlot that spread across the back of both family's land. And, Charlie Yates—Charlie Yates *wrapped his big arms around his ma*. What the fuck are his big arms doin' on my ma? Jimmy remembers thinking, beginning to feel desperate. Then, *they kissed!* Charlie Yates kissed his ma or did *she* kiss *him*? By then, Jimmy was getting light-headed and his thoughts were getting mushy.

His ma and Charlie went into the cabin. Jimmy crept toward it. He got to a little window on the side and peeked in. There they were standing in front of a potbelly iron stove, with their faces *and* bodies stuck together. Jimmy thought he was going to heave.

That cabin wasn't like a house. You could stand outside and hear everything that was being said inside. They had stopped kissing but she kept running her hands over his hefty body as he asked, "Did you get Jimmy the one that I picked out?"

She said, "It's in Rose's barn."

He said, "It's the Yamaha 175. Right? Do you need any more money?"

She said, "*Yes*, it's the 175 and no, *honey*, what you gave me more than covered it. I used the extra to get him some new sneakers—the kind he's been hinting around for. He's going to have his best birthday ever, thanks again to his *father.*"

Jimmy knew he was going to be sick. His head was spinning— really spinning—like in some movie about demonic possession. Either his head was spinning or the whole world was spinning around him while he stood still at the core of it. Either way, Jimmy knew he had to stop the spinning. And he knew instantly that he was going to do it by blowing them away. He went to the house and got the gun. But he saw those coyotes—killed them instead. And, then, he went back to sit on "Alice" to figure out what to do next.

As he runs his fingers over his car's steering wheel, Jimmy remembers running his hands around the smooth metal steering wheel on his granpap's tractor. He remembers when he was a little kid sitting close to his granpap on the tractor loving all of the smells belching out of "Alice".

Jimmy had sat there remembering the first time he steered the Allis-Chalmers—his first memory. He, Will and Terry were all over to his Aunt Rose's house with his ma—so she could borrow something. They borrow back and forth and then gripe about it because everyone is keeping count and nothing is never, ever, *even*—nothing never is, Jimmy thinks.

Granpap had told Lizzie Jo, who had the baby bouncing in her lap, that he was taking this whipper snapper back to their house with him on "Alice". He called his tractor, "Alice" and all his grandkids, whipper snappers. Lizzie had protested that Jimmy was too little—that he might fall off the tractor and "get runned over." "Well, I s'pose he could," Granpap had said as he grabbed Jimmy and hauled him out there to the Allis-Chalmers on his hip parallel to the ground like a sack of potatoes. "Alice" looked spectacular to Jimmy. But she must have been old and beat up even then.

Granpap had spread his legs and plunked Jimmy on the front edge of the metal seat that poked out from under Granpap. Jimmy had put his hands on the steering wheel and believed for a long time that he alone had steered that tractor all the way home. Granpap had turned him into a monster about driving the thing. He wanted to drive it all the time after that which he didn't even get to *pretend* to do for another several years. Granpap was like that. He loved to get you hooked on something and then take it away. He'd show you something, get you all worked up about it, and then smack you for wanting it. Eugene's done the same thing a few times—more than a few times.

Jimmy had sat there on that old tractor wondering what he should feel since he was about to kill himself? He knew by then that he was not going to kill them or he'd be rushing back out there to catch them in the act, so they could be found naked, doing it in Charlie Yates's old hunting shack that Will and Jimmy had both been told explicitly to stay away from. Lizzie Jo had made that perfectly clear. She got wild about it when Jimmy was about seven. She was hanging clothes on the line. Jimmy remembers this perfectly. He was standing beside the basket beating the ground with a stick, trying to hit ants. His ma had said, "Where you been all mornin'?" She wasn't mad. She sounded happy. Jimmy got one ant with that stick real good. He got down on his knees to watch it writhe while a few others darted up to it and then went about their business.

Jimmy had poked at the ant with his finger. His face was real close to the "good earth" as Granpap called it. Jimmy always liked the smell of dirt. "We found this hideout back in the woods. We're going to make it a fort," he'd said, amazed that another ant had picked up the writhing one and was carrying it a few steps in one direction and then in another like it couldn't figure out which way to go—where to take the hurt ant—what to do. At one point, the carrying ant had dropped the hurt one. Then the carrying ant had struggled again to hoist it up and struggled to move it.

All of a sudden Jimmy had felt sorry that he'd hit it with the stick. He had thought of his little brother and of the ambulance and the volunteer firemen. He'd remembered his ma laying crumpled in the grass. His dad was in a rage running around the barnyard bare-chested in November with a couple of men chasing after him trying to slow him down and when they did, they poured some liquor down his throat. His dad had torn off his flannel shirt popping every button. Jimmy remembers standing alone watching all of this, not knowing what to do. No one had seemed to notice him. He was alone—like standing in the eye of a tornado until Charlie Yates had swept him up in his big arms and said, "You're all right son. Your Daddy will keep you safe." He'd held him close and patted his back as Jimmy's little arms wrapped themselves around Charlie's thick neck. Jimmy knew what to do—hang on—*no matter what*—**HANG ON!**

For a long time Charlie had walked him around the barnyard or sat on the porch swing. Jimmy didn't look at him or loosen his grip. He didn't even know on whose barrel chest he was clinging. Jimmy had wet his pants because he wouldn't let go of that neck for nothing. Charlie continued walking or swinging for hours with Jimmy's urine down the front of his overalls. Finally, Aunt Rose had come home from the hospital and pulled him off Charlie. Then Jimmy was able to see who he'd been stuck to—a fat, red-faced guy who kept calling him "son," kissing his neck and patting his back.

Little Jimmy had wondered that day when he watched the ants under the clothesline if that one ant that was carrying the other one was like the volunteer firemen trying to make Terry get alive or was he a Charlie Yates ant carrying Jimmy around—little Jimmy—who felt like he'd been hit that day by a giant's big stick.

Jimmy's face was only about three inches from those ants when his ma had grabbed him by the back of his neck and had pushed his face into the grass and had said in a voice Jimmy has never heard from her before or since, *"Don't you ever, never go near that cabin again."* She'd scared Jimmy. She'd made him cry and run into the house to the cubby hole under the cellar stair where he had shook and cried. For several days after, his ma would look at him with the witchiest eyes and he knew what they were saying, *don't you ever, never go back to that cabin again* and unbelievably, he didn't until the *fateful night* a year ago last October.

"Jimmy," Starr says softly. Jimmy opens his eyes to see Starr with hers closed. Her full lips barely separate as she says, "Wake me up in a little bit. Okay?" Then, her head droops toward the window. They've had the engine running for heat. Jimmy gets worried that maybe they're both getting killed by fumes, which last week he wouldn't have minded, but now, he's got this book going. So, he cracks the window a little and then a little more. He doesn't shut off the engine. Starr would get cold.

59

I didn't kill the whore or that fuckin' farmer, he thinks while he picks at a piece of vinyl that's about to come off the dashboard. He didn't say a thing to anyone except Starr when he finally got it all figured out enough to even talk about. It took several months of thinking before he finally got it all pieced together.

He had wrecked that bike but good by running it off a dock and into a swimming hole on his Aunt Rose and Uncle Kink's farm down the road. Killed it dead when it was brand new! Said it was an accident which Eugene had a hard time believing and tried to ground him for six weeks. Lizzie openly overruled Eugene for the second time in their marriage. The first was when she went ahead and bought that Yamaha after Eugene told her not to. Eugene harped at Lizzie who was brokenhearted over that dirt bike. He'd said Jimmy didn't need that bike anyway and she'd wasted their money *as usual!* Two months later Aunt Rose gave Travis's old car to Jimmy since Travis wasn't going to be needing a car for quite a while. Even when he gets out he isn't going to be needing it because he'll be wearing an ankle bracelet that will monitor him to make sure he's staying home for another six months.

Jimmy did kill those dogs, of course, which he went out to look at the next day. He killed Cindy Mead's Marilyn which had her name and address on a tag on the red collar. He thought the other one was hers, too, so when his dad told him the next month to get rid of Will's dog, Slime, and while he was at it dump that good-for-nothing beagle which wouldn't hunt for him or he'd kill them both that night, Jimmy did his good deed and saved those dog's asses by giving them to Mrs. Mead to replace the ones he'd killed. That part worked out all nice and neat until he went to Cindy's house and saw that picture and heard her talk about that dog. No way is he *ever* going to tell her what happened.

When he saw those dog bodies the next day, he *did* feel sorry. He'll admit that but he was still reeling about his ma and Charlie Yates—about why Charlie would buy him a brand new dirt bike and the reference to "his father." He didn't give another thought to those dogs until the other day at Cindy Mead's house.

Jimmy dragged those dogs up to the pig pit where his dad throws dead pigs and shoveled enough lime on them that you couldn't tell one carcass from another. First, he took the collar off the only one that had a collar—the little one named Marilyn. He threw the collar in the weeds near the silo.

Starr jumps up in her seat as she wakes up, scared over some dream she had about wigs made of dead people's hair. "I'd better get home," she says as she yawns real big.

Man, she's so sexy, Dack agonizes as he turns the ignition key, pumps the petal. His engine races.

Four

Sunday morning pancakes bubble in the black iron skillet that Lizzie Jo inherited when her ma went to live in Anderson, Indiana with her ma's sister, Wilma. "Won't be needin' two black iron pots," Wilma had said. Will is in Indiana with Lizzie Jo's ma. He's trying to get his GED. They're probably spoiling him with gooey desserts every night. Just what he needs, Lizzie thinks. Two fat old ladies spoilin' him—and she means it. He got nothin' good from any of us, she's come to think.

Give him a little rope and he'll hang himself, Eugene was always saying to explain why he was so hard on Will—as though that was an explanation. Eugene's rope nearly strangled that kid. Lizzie figures he was hard on him because he saw himself in Will.

Lizzie knew in her heart that she favored Jimmy. She loved him more because of *whose* he was but she never told anybody anything—not even her sister Rose—although Rose knew something without knowing what. Lizzie thinks it's a wonder everybody doesn't know *what.* Look at the kid! Eugene is short, skinny, puny, even at forty-two. Will's built like him and then, there's Jimmy, big and muscular. Maybe that's why Eugene has laid off Jimmy for several years—he could tell Jimmy would grow up to be bigger than himself and do to Eugene what had been done to him.

Lizzie flips the cakes over and stands there at the stove with her left hand on her lower back and the spatula in her right. She looks out the window, off toward the cabin, and a softness enters her being. She shakes her head and wonders how she's kept this lie for so many years. Her eyes tear. She blinks several times as a way of getting her emotions under control.

Jimmy shuffles into the room and plops down in his chair at the table covered with a plastic table cloth printed with old-fashioned coffee grinders. She doesn't look over but she knows exactly how he looks—moody, angry. "These pancakes will be ready in a minute," she says. It's then that she looks over at her moody, angry boy.

Fuckin' whore, Jimmy thinks. I oughta tell dad. Dad would take care of you and Charlie. It has been over a year since he saw them in that cabin and nine months since he put it all together—that Charlie is his real dad. Jimmy's still mad. But, he hasn't told anyone except Starr and Cindy Mead what he knows.

He can't wait to get out of here. Not just out of here today but forever. He hates his ma and his dad and Charlie Yates and this house and Christmas and every fucking thing. And he hates himself and the stupid things he does. He hates how he thinks that getting his story told will help him stop hating everybody and everything. He hates how he keeps driving by Charlie Yates's house, slowly, trying to look at him, and how a couple of times Charlie was out in the yard looking back. Something funny had happened for a second when Jimmy and Charlie's eyes met. Jimmy couldn't tell exactly what had happened but it sucked, whatever it was. Jimmy had gunned it at that point as though he'd done a drive-by *shooting,* when all it was was a drive-by *viewing.*

He hates how last spring he had gone to the back of the property (skirting around that fucking cabin) to watch Charlie plowing a field. He'd laid in the weeds in a drainage ditch and watched him go around and around, back and forth—whatever Charlie was doing—he'd watched *him*—nothing else. Jesus, he thinks, I did it again last month. Jimmy was feeding the pigs when he'd heard Charlie's corn picker in his west field. He'd dropped everything and went running back there. God, *he hates doing that!* It's sick, man, really sick, Jimmy believes, to go running like that.

Charlie's pretty fucking old for his ma. What does she see in him, anyway? He's fat, bald and red in the face like he's sunburned all year long. His wife had died the spring before Jimmy caught him with his ma. Jimmy wonders how many years his ma and Charlie have been doing this? He's sixteen—so, sixteen at least! Sick, man. That's what Jimmy thinks. Fuckin' sick!

Jimmy hates the stupid thoughts he gets. He hates those more than anything. Like when he thinks about that day when he was little and his arms were wrapped around Charlie's neck and how it felt like they fit there, perfectly. God, he hates those kind of thoughts. Makes him want to heave.

With her face half-turned toward her bedroom, Lizzie yells, "Eugene, the pancakes are almost done!"

"Jimmy," she says, "get three plates, will ya?" Then, she goes over to the silverware drawer knowing full well that Jimmy will not move out of that slouch. He's been nasty to her for a year. Before that they got along well. But Lizzie has seen her sisters go through this with their kids and they come out the other end okay—except Travis. He's been in the Juvenile Detention Center over a year for taking that car stereo, those guns and all of the other stuff they found in Rose's old chicken house.

Lizzie feels like going back to bed and staying there for a couple of lifetimes. She stayed there for a good bit, once, long ago in some yesterday—back there at that time when her life was a complete blur. When it was like trying to drive in a downpour with broken wipers and it wasn't as though she ever got the wipers going, she merely stopped driving for a while until the rain quit. If anything like that happens to her again, that will be "it." Even if she had Charlie at her side, she'd be "done for." Oh, god, *Charlie*... She thinks, *my Charlie*. If anything happens to Charlie ... She can't ever finish that thought whenever it comes up.

What would she do? How would she mourn her secret lover, the father of her child? Could she cry at the funeral? She had gone to his wife's. She'd stayed in the back and tried not to look at Charlie. She was afraid he'd be looking back and then everyone would know when their eyes met. Charlie doesn't know how to hide what he's thinking or feeling. He lights up when he sees her in the hardware or getting gas at Buddy's. Sometimes, she thinks he wants them to get caught—especially now that Sarah's gone.

Poor, Sarey. It took her two years to die after they found the cancer. Lizzie had heard from Edna, the cashier at Buddy's that the doctors thought they'd got it all. Then a year-and-a-half later Lizzie heard from Brownie Herguson at the bank that it was back. Lizzie had to hear about it from others because Charlie had told Lizzie right off the bat, as soon as they found it, that he couldn't see her any more—*guilt!*

Charlie had called Lizzie from the hospital—called her right at work where she's not supposed to get or make personal phone calls unless it's an emergency. Boy was her heart pounding hard when she'd walked into the office to get that call! Of course, she couldn't say much anything back to Charlie because Carla, Stephanie and Tony were all in the office. She'd said, "Okay" several times and "Thank-you for calling. Good-bye." When she handed the handset back to Carla who looked curious, Lizzie had said, "Sorry. It was one of Jimmy's teachers. Problem at school." Then, she'd chuckled a little, nervously, when what she needed to do was collapse in a heap on the floor and cry her eyes out.

On the way back to her station, she'd agonized over her loss and about how guilty Charlie felt about Sarey. He'd told her from that pay phone at the hospital that no matter what, if Lizzie really needed him—if Eugene got mean to any of them, to call him or come get him. She didn't—not that she didn't want or need to.

She'd liked to die getting that call that day! And she had to go back to mixing dough like it was nothing. "It ain't nothin'," she'd yelled across to Ethel when she got back to her vat. Ethel had a concerned look on her face. She knows Liz's "tragic history" as Ethel refers to Terry's being killed.

That call was the beginning of a two year drought. Lizzie didn't even get to say good-bye to Charlie except on the phone and she'd said it like he was anybody. She realizes, now, that you never get to say good-bye—they're usually gone before the good-byes get said. That's the way it always seems to happen. It happened that way with—Terry, Will, Charlie and her own father. That's the way it happened to Eugene when his dad died, and years earlier when his ma left. She'd left in the middle of the night, they'd heard, with some guy named Julius from South Carolina, and they'd never seen her again.

Lizzie Jo had thought she'd gotten over Charlie—thought she'd learned to live okay without him after a long, tormented period of time. But a week after Sarah's funeral, she'd paced the floor in the kitchen and couldn't stop tidying up. She had emptied the crumbs from the toaster. She'd wiped up the countertops more than once, even back behind the mixer and the ceramic pig cookie jar where she hadn't looked in a while. She'd arranged the mugs on the mug tree that Will had made in shop so they were all facing the same way.

Finally, Lizzie realized she was going to see Charlie. She hadn't been there or talked to Charlie in two years except for chance encounters at the bank, the gas station. Places like that. She'd gone to the refrigerator, scooped some rice pudding out into a Tupperware container and sat it on the counter. She'd gone upstairs and checked on Will. He hadn't been chased off to Indiana, yet. He was asleep upstairs in his front bedroom. She always checked on Will. He was the light sleeper and the problem child with that gun of his, shooting at anything that moves. When he was six, Lizzie had caught him ripping the wings off butterflies. When he was ten, he'd put lighted firecrackers down the throats of toads and frogs to blow them up.

Lizzie peered across the hall into Jimmy's room that night. He was flung across his bed at an odd angle with his covers half on the floor. She'd descended the stairs and listened through her bedroom door for Eugene's snores. When Eugene goes to sleep, she's safe until morning. He sleeps like a rock. She figures it's the whiskey that he downs every night about an hour before he goes to bed. Lizzie couldn't wake him up even if there was a fire. That doesn't worry her.

Lizzie had grabbed the Tupperware container from the counter and headed out into the spring air, hoping desperately to be wrapped again in Charlie's warm arms. That night, she'd walked past the cabin and went straight for the house.

Charlie and Sarah never had kids. Sarah had miscarried a lot but there was one full-term, live birth. The baby was more than likely severely retarded, according to the doctors. They'd named her Patricia Marie. She'd died in three days. Sarey got real distant after that and decided there would be no more chances for children and, according to Charlie, she wouldn't talk about it, just moved to another bedroom. She wouldn't go any farther away than that and she wouldn't let Charlie go. She didn't believe in divorce. So, she acted to the rest of the world as though everything was normal. She did her gardening and canning. She went to church. She had a yard full of flowers. Everybody thought Charlie and Sarah

67

were happy together. But at night she shut herself up in her room and locked the door.

The farm has been in Charlie's family from way back. He loves that land. Only he's so frustrated that he talks of selling, since there's no one he can legitimately leave it to except some nieces and a nephew who live in the northeast, and they're Sarah's people. Charlie doesn't really know them. He talks of moving to Florida or Arizona. He says his arthritis is bothering him. Lizzie thinks he's trying to pressure her—that he may go ahead and leave her. How could she live without him being back there behind her? She figures she'll be left at some point under any circumstances since he's twenty years older—although you never know about life. She knows that better than many—that you *never* know! Lord, Lizzie thinks, Lord, Lord, how could she get by if Charlie wasn't somewhere on this earth? She'd learned to live without him for two years but just knowing that he was back there in the house behind hers gave her comfort. She had something to look forward to—hope.

Lizzie puts the plate of pancakes in the middle of the table and an empty plate in front of Jimmy. She goes to the back door and yells, "Eugene! Your pancakes are ready!" She'd forgotten he'd gone out to do some early chores. He sticks his hand in the air but goes on tinkering with something resting against a saw horse. Lizzie tries to shut the door. It's stuck at the bottom until she lifts up on it as she swings it shut.

Jimmy takes four pancakes drowning them in syrup, much of which will be left on the plate when he's finished. She'll give what's left on Jimmy's plate to the stray dog she started calling Pepper. "Tell your dad they're in there," she says as she covers the rest of the pancakes and slides them in the oven, turning it on warm. She goes in the front room to sit in the rocker by the picture window.

This rocker is so quiet, she thinks, not a sound and it's not a creeper, either. Not now. Not then. She had rocked all her babies in this rocker, ignorant of what life would do to them, to her.

Things are so fragile between she and Jimmy. And Eugene is so peculiar. Sometimes downright mean—hard to love but he's done good considering what he came from. His ma was a wicked woman. She'd hit those kids across the face as soon as look at them. Everybody was glad when she ran off. They think she lives in Florida. No letters, no cards, no phone calls, just hearsay.

All the kids in that family are messed up. Eugene's done better than the other two. Gerald is in prison at Marquette. Been up there since Eugene was sixteen. When Gerald was nineteen and living up north, he raped a police officer's little girl, slit her throat and threw her out in a ditch to die. The police officer said he'd make sure Gerald never got paroled. Eugene wonders why some convict hasn't killed him. They hate child molesters in prison since most of them know all about it from the kid's point of view. Nobody mentions Gerald any more. He's dead to Eugene, essentially Sis is, too.

Sis has been married for sure twice and has four kids by four different men. One of them was a biker named Skin who had tattoos all over his body. He was her last husband and the father of her last kid. Skin was the best dad Sis ever got for those kids but she dumped him, took the kids and moved to Tennessee with a guy named Rexall Horton. Because Eugene was the only one who stayed, he got the family farm.

The Christmas tree stands in the corner where one has been every year since Lizzie married Eugene and moved in. On the top is the crocheted white angel her mother made from directions in a *Family Circle* magazine.

Lizzie rocks and looks out across the road into the woods. Sometimes, they see deer out there. One morning, when it was misty and foggy and it was just getting light, she was sitting in this rocker, sipping her coffee when she saw a doe walk right onto the gravel road with a younger one trailing behind. Usually deer are on the alert, wound up like a spring watching for danger especially during deer season. This one's head hung low and it didn't act quite right. It shouldn't have been walking so slowly, so close to the house, out in the open. Something was wrong. It was beautiful, sleek with dark "doe" eyes and the young one still had that baby look to its form.

The doe didn't look injured but how could Lizzie tell? All she knew was that the deer wasn't limping and she couldn't see any blood or holes—but a bullet hole could be real small, couldn't it? It could have had gangrene in a wound. Once Eugene brought home a deer to butcher that had puss filled holes from older bullet wounds. Once she saw one running with an arrow stuck in its shoulder. She knew that one was slowly bleeding to death.

Finally, Lizzie came to the conclusion that the deer in their road was exhausted from running and hiding and trying to survive along with her baby. It was like she'd given up. Lizzie would have given anything if she could have offered them refuge in the barn until the end of deer season. The only thing she could do was make sure Eugene didn't see the doe since he had a doe permit and had been trying to get himself a deer for nearly a week.

There are some things that are always in your mind. Lizzie knows that. No matter what's going on, what she's doing— those kids are always there. She still has Will and Jimmy to worry about. Little Terry is in her memories. She doesn't have to worry about him. She knows that he's safe with Jesus.

She remembers nothing of that exact moment when she had realized Terry was dead. She remembers the moment she saw he'd been run over. The whole realization probably lasted about three seconds, which had seemed like an hour at the time. It's true that time slows down instantly. She was seeing and moving in slow motion. Now, it screams through her mind in her sleep like a freight train in the night. She feels it coming through blackness with a rumbling rush that gets more and more intense until there are flashes like sparks off a track. Then it's gone, back into the night, into the black.

Will came running into the house to call the fire department, she remembers that. She remembers Jimmy standing near the pickup looking bewildered, sucking his first two fingers in his mouth. She remembers thinking, I thought he gave that up a couple of years ago. No one but Charlie ever asked her what she had seen of the baby laying there on the ground. He told her that she should talk about what she saw. Nobody had wanted to talk about it but Charlie. She thought he was horribly cruel to ask her to remember it or bloodthirsty to want to hear it, but he'd kept prodding and poking until she'd screamed at him and went berserk and spit it out of the recesses of her mind where she'd stuck it because nobody but Charlie wanted to hear about that part—not even her. He was right to force her to get it out of her because it was always going to be there anyway, even if she didn't look at it.

"Blood," she had screamed while Charlie gripped her by her cold arms. "Blood out his mouth . . . ears, blood . . . eyes, blank, gone . . . Terry . . . crushed . . . chest crushed . . . cowboy hat . . . cold . . . blackness."

They had taken her to the hospital in the same ambulance as Terry. No one had worked on him. He was under a blanket. They were doing something to her. She can't remember what.

Lizzie remembers that when they'd arrived at the emergency room, she began begging to see Terry whom they'd taken right away to the morgue. The police officer and several others had tried to convince her otherwise but she was adamant and causing a scene. So they'd led her down a long hall. Rose had propped her up on one side and some officer on the other. Eugene couldn't even stand up by then so he certainly couldn't have gone down the hall. He had called her a *wimp* so many times because of things she couldn't stand to watch, like the time he had dropped baby mice which he was holding by the tail into the mouths of the barn cats who were swirling around below. He had called her a wimp for finding his cruelty despicable.

Someone had opened a big steel-gray door. The officer at her side had walked her over to a table with a sheet. She could hear Rose back by the door, crying. "Now don't pull this sheet down any farther," some guy in green said as he'd uncovered the face of her little baby boy.

"It's a healthy baby boy," they'd said that June in the delivery room. Lizzie was disappointed. After two boys she wanted a girl. Rose had told her that because of the way she was carrying that time, it was going to be a girl. When, they'd said "boy," Lizzie was disappointed. Everyone always says, "Oh, you're just so happy to have a healthy baby that it doesn't matter when they say it's the one you weren't wanting." But, Lizzie *was* disappointed.

She hadn't really wanted this child. She was through with two children. But, Eugene had forbidden her to get her tubes tied and he wouldn't get a vasectomy because he said it was an unnatural thing to do. Terry was a *mistake*, as they say, and a boy. She'd named him Terry because she was going to name her little girl, Theresa June. She'd named him Terry Lee and within a day, everyone was right, it didn't matter. She was in love!

Rose was there when Terry was born. They couldn't find Eugene. He was in town somewhere and had gone all the way home. When they got ahold of him, it was all over. Terry had come fast. Rose was with her there in Reed County Hospital that June. And, she was with her there again that Saturday. In November. In the morgue.

Those remembered moments in that room down on the lower level of the hospital are crystal clear, not fuzzy like right after it happened at the farm or fuzzy like the months that followed. Those moments at the hospital are hard-edged, cold like the stainless steel that had surrounded her.

Lizzie had performed a ritual of some sort, like Holy Communion or Baptism and it was as though she knew exactly how to do it—not like she'd done it before in some other life. It was like something built into her from birth. An instinct passed though the ages. How to do something horrible that has to be done. How to say good-bye to your dead child.

She'd felt like one of those dark-skinned women with fabric draped around her body and over her head, one of those gaunt, empty-eyed drought victims on the nightly news who is holding in her arms her child who has died of starvation, one of those women who doesn't notice the flies at the corner of her eyes, drinking tear drops from her body before they even form.

Lizzie had bent over, put her face close to Terry's. She'd cupped the palm of her right hand around Terry's cheek. She'd run her fingers through what she could of his hair which was matted with dried blood. She'd cupped his face with both hands. She'd kissed him on the forehead. If she'd had a hankie, she would have spit on it and wiped the blood off his face like her ma did when she was little. She'd wished she could bathe him, clean him up, dress him. That's her job. She's his mother. Her kids were always clean. They didn't always have new clothes, but they were clean.

She'd told Terry she loved him. She'd told him that he'd be her baby *forever.* She'd put her hand on his chest, motionless beneath the sheet—*he's not asleep!*—oh, Jesus, God in heaven, *my baby's not asleep!* His chest was caved in. She'd retracted her hand from his chest when she felt it. She'd bent down again and with the other hand across his forehead, Lizzie whispered in his ear: *"Jesus loves you, this I know for the bible tells me so. Little ones to him belong, for they are weak but he is strong."*

Lizzie had kissed him again, and then she'd stood up straight. She'd felt strong, almost powerful, though she couldn't understand why. The officer had taken her arm and said, "We should go now." She'd let him lead her off and back down that long, florescent hall. The lights were blinding her—so bright. It was like the one they'd described on TV when someone told the story of having died and come back to life. She wasn't crying. She could hear every step they each took and every echo of every step. She can still hear them to this day. The closer they'd gotten to the end of the hall, the weaker she had become until she'd collapsed back into life.

Eugene comes in the back door and goes to the bathroom to wash up. She hopes he doesn't holler at her to eat with him.

Today is gray but the sun's supposed to shine later and no more snow. That's what they said on WJR. It was gray the day they buried Terry. There are a lot of gray days in Michigan. She's been told this by people she works with who have lived other places. Lizzie has never lived any other place so gray in the winter seems normal to her. She's within a mile of where she grew up and Eugene is in the same house in which he lived when he got on her school bus, second stop after her house. When he was seventeen, he got a car and picked her up every day. Lizzie was fourteen years old.

Contrary to what everyone thought, Eugene never got anything out of her—at least not intercourse—until after he came home from the army and they had decided they were engaged. In high school, Lizzie wasn't very interested in Eugene in that way, all she wanted was to be able to say she had a boyfriend with a car and Eugene didn't really press it too much until he got home from the service. Lizzie had ⋯'d been doing it over there in Germany and ⋯sistent. She was ready by then

⋯arried she didn't want sex with him ⋯they'd done in the back seat of his ⋯nent, she resisted him until that one ⋯the wedding. Lizzie's heart beats ⋯about it—how she'd finally submitted. ⋯ting, but she probably deserved it. ⋯did deserve what she got. Didn't she?

⋯couple—joined together for better or for ⋯ted to be a *wife*. She had a duty. It was ⋯room next door! He was her problem. ⋯orny as hell. He'd touched her breast ⋯while she was frying ham for everybody ⋯e were engaged. He reached out and put ⋯zie almost died.

⋯onth, he got her alone in the bathroom— came in when ⋯ e was fixing her hair, shut the door, and before she knew what was happening, he was rubbing his crotch on her backside and telling her how good her hair smelled. It made her sick but she'd felt sorry for the old man. He'd been through a lot. Still, it was a relief when he'd died six years later of a massive cerebral hemorrhage of the brain. They said he was dead before he hit the ground back there in the orchard. Eugene had said it was good he didn't die with the pigs. They'd have been nibbling on him before he was found! Lizzie thinks that's probably true, the way the old man loved hitting those pigs across the snout with that old silver baton of Sis's.

Eugene had discovered early in the marriage that he liked to be rough when they had sex. What he really wanted was her to be rough with him. She couldn't. So *he* hurt *her*. It turned him on. And when she didn't make a sound because of his father being in the next room, it made him want to hurt her more. She had told Charlie about it. He was all set to go kill Eugene. Lizzie had managed to defuse him. Charlie knows how to make love. Charlie calls her his *Lady Elizabeth*.

She's not sure but she thinks Will came out of the night Eugene had finally forced himself on her or it could have been the next one or the one after that. Will came from one of those black-and-blue nights.

Lizzie stops rocking. What's left of her coffee is cold in the mug. Did anyone else feel it that day? Lizzie wonders. Did anyone else feel that little current of air that had lifted her skirt that day at the cemetery as it filtered through the gaps in the gathering of family and friends around her baby's casket. It was on its way to some other place—far away where the sky is always blue—where Elizabeth Josephine Trueberry has never been and will never be. It had felt warm, dry, fresh cutting against the dampness of fall. It was a little breeze from summer lagging way behind but heading south. It had felt like a premonition and now she's afraid it really was.

Did they feel it, she asks herself, again? She had tried to look at the faces in the crowd, but she sensed they were all staring at her. She was being studied. *She* studied one spot on the little casket, a place where the stain was darker. Their eyes were asking—*what is it like to lose a child . . . in that way?* Eugene supported Lizzie with his arm under her elbow. Her arm felt like a spear resting in the crook of Eugene's. **She—wanted—to—stab—him—with—it!**

It was an accident. She knows that. She knew that even then, but she'd wanted them all to wonder. Eugene is the type of man to wonder about. "When a child dies," the minister had said. Lizzie remembers thinking, did a child die? "When a child dies," he had said, "it is a tragedy—a parent's greatest sorrow."

Lizzie gets up from the rocker. Eugene is yelling for her to come eat breakfast with him and she will, and then Rose will pick her up for church and, then around ten o'clock tonight when Eugene is snoring and Jimmy's tucked away upstairs, Elizabeth will walk out her back door, past the barn and down the lane. She will walk past the cabin, to Charlie's house and up the stairs to his bedroom. She won't be able to stop herself. She won't try.

Five

Starr is upstairs sleeping late as Steve watches Joan out the window. She's meditating on the bench by the lily pond that she had dug three or four years ago. She's always making improvements in the place—dramatic improvements like the little lights that line the front sidewalk which come on automatically at dusk and go off at midnight, and the deck with the Polynesian theme hot tub and the "entertainment" room. Steve gets stuck on that name, "entertainment" room. Why can't she call it the basement. That's what it is, after all, a walk-out basement. But she teaches theater out at the college. She's into "pretend." Steve figured that out a long time ago.

Steve's mom never knew she had an "entertainment" room. She thought she had a cellar with a Ping-Pong table over by the furnace that ate Ping-Pong balls. That's where his dad used to *entertain* Steve and his brother up against the wall, with *the belt*. "To the cellar!" he'd bellow at one or the other, as he snapped his belt, getting everybody in the house worked up.

While he's still watching Joan, Steve dials the phone, but before he hears it ring, he hangs up. Bad idea, he thinks. His hand is still on the receiver when Starr pads down the stairs in her nightgown, plops on the other end of the sectional and punches on the TV with the remote. She flips past three preachers—one with the most pained look on his face and his arms waving back and forth above his head.

"Lord," he implores, *"we know we have siiiiiiiiinned!"* She flips past a show with people testifying religiously about a teeth whitening gel. Steve's irritated. "You know there's nothing good on at this time on Sunday!" he tells Starr as she settles on a panel discussion about urban planning that Steve thinks can't possibly interest her. He looks over at her. Her big unblinking eyes are glued to the screen, like she's in a trance. Her feet are tucked under her nightgown. Her mass of brown hair is pulled into a wild ponytail. Tendrils, that escape, fall loosely from her temples. Steve doesn't like what just passed through his mind. He looks away, quickly. Nothing like that should dare enter any father's mind. All he thought in essence was God, how did his little girl get to be this *thing*—attractive, young woman. He can't bring himself to think it in those words—too scary on too many fronts. Did he think something wrong? He's not sure.

Steve is becoming uncomfortable with Starr. She'd come out of her bedroom this past summer, and walked right past him to the refrigerator, wearing little bikini panties with tiny, pink rose buds printed on them and a little t-shirt that didn't even cover her middle. He had barked at her about cleaning Romeo's litter pan, and then told Joan to tell her to not walk around the house like that—"She's getting too old to be so immodest." Starr had come back at him later saying that what she had on was not *underwear* just *sleepwear* and besides she had more covered than when she goes swimming. Steve had made a mental note to discuss that swimsuit with Joan.

Steve never knows anything about what's happening around here. That's okay. They don't know what's going on with the business. It's a mutual lack of interest, but sometimes it makes him damn mad to come home and find that something's been changed. Like when Joan had moved that little table by the door and he'd come in to fling his brief case to the right as he'd done for years and it had crashed to the floor (his secretary pulls stuff like that, too) or when Starr became a

79

woman—so to speak—and Joan didn't bother to tell him. When he had figured it out, *he* almost crashed to the floor thinking that his little girl could actually have a baby.

Steve looks over at her and wishes he'd spent more time with his bright little Starr. Life is flying by. His smoky gray eyes get moist when he thinks about it. Starr will be all grown up and gone before he knows it. He looks at her skinny little body and remembers when Joan was skinny—not that she's fat now but she's not skinny. She's got a little pouch she's carrying around in the front and a couple of bags on the sides of her thighs and the roundness has "gone south" as he puts it.

Then he's no beauty either. Come to think of it, he hasn't really looked at himself in several months. For a while he studied himself in the mirror a lot and "preened" in the bathroom every morning. It's different, now. He feels tired. All of the time, he . . . feels . . . tired. It's really hard to get up in the morning. Maybe because he spends half the night, every night, dozing right here on this sectional with Romeo, his buddy, but that's not *sound* sleeping. Romeo insists on laying on Steve's chest and he weighs in at 15 pounds. The males in this house have to stick together, he thinks, even though Romeo is neutered. Shit, I might as well be, too, Steve thinks . . . for all the action around here, I might as well be, too, he thinks again.

It really pisses Joan off that he goes to sleep on this couch. One night she came screaming down here—out of control and started beating on him with a pillow. God, what would the men in the board room at the bank think of that? It's pretty damn humiliating to get pounded on by your wife.

Steve glares down at his stomach under his t-shirt. How the hell did that pile of blubber get there? He'd lost a whole bunch of it last year. Hell, he had a pretty damn flat gut for a guy his age. Cindy told him so. She liked to feel it—sometimes she'd punch at it, a play-punch, and he'd stand there like Hercules with his head thrown back, his hands on his hips and his stomach muscles all tight. Then he'd grab his Cindy and throw her on the bed and have his way with her . . . Hell, the truth is once she got beyond her insecurity, *she* practically *took him* every time. She was wild in bed.

Did he really do that? Carry on for over a year with a woman who lives in the same community? Hell, he wasn't *carrying on*—he was in love—crazy in love as well as lust. Sometimes he surprised himself in that bed in room five out at the Tidy View. God, that Cindy, she was starved. He would *never* tell anyone this—he was damned starved, too.

Steve looks down again. He can't get over the gut he's looking at. He takes his two hands and grabs it between his thumbs and fingers and wads it up like a big beach ball. Starr looks over and says, "Oh, gross, Daaaaad!" She says the "Dad" all whiny. Steve keeps a firm grip on the lard and says, "Just think, someday, if you're real lucky like your mother, you'll be married to a rich guy with one of these."

"I don't think that's funny!" Starr says as she marches up the stairs.

I don't either, Steve thinks. No guy had better lay a hand on you or I'll kill him.

That's it! Steve heads up the stairs to put on his jogging pants and jacket. Joan is in the kitchen when Steve comes out of the bedroom jogging already, he stops to jog in place while taking a bite out of Joan's muffin, right off of her plate. "Going jogging," he announces, already puffing a little.

"Where?" Joan queries. "There's snow all over the ground."

"On the road! It's plowed."

"Yes, but—"

Shit, Steve thinks, still jogging in place, here it comes—a volley of her famous "yes buts." Steve knows in his heart he could come close to killing over these "yes buts" and he's pretty sure any jury of his peers, all married men, of course, (well-to-do, married men with girlfriends) would let him off on justified homicide, if there is such a thing or an insanity plea. It's moments like these he can't wait to be hard of hearing like his dad. He'll stick his finger in his ear and twist that little knob on the hearing aid—like the old man does to Steve's mom.

Joan's voice screeches back into his consciousness . . . "and the snow is heaped up on the side of the road. How are you going to get off when cars come by? You might get hit like that runner who got hit by the drunk driver in the middle of the day—if you don't have a *coronary* first."

She's digging, he thinks. She doesn't believe him about the chest pains. Just because the EKG didn't show anything when he went to that specialist and ran on the treadmill. They'll all be sorry when I drop dead, he thinks. Steve feels that it's too bad he won't be around to say, "I told you so." So, his only satisfaction is to lay the groundwork for future guilt—when Joan can think of this moment and feel terrible for years and years to come. And so, he says, "Do I detect some glee at your thought of my having a heart attack?" He doesn't wait for a response. "Anyway, the only ones out now are the Christians on their way to church and they're supposedly sober and not exactly in a race to get to their pew despite what they profess."

With that he runs out of the house, down the driveway and to the right. He jogs until he's out of sight of the house. He stops and bends over at the waist with his hands on his knees and tries to catch his breath. When he does he saunters on down the road feeling goddamn tired and thinking that female strangers don't look at him like they used to unless he's getting out of that "hot-shot" car of his, as his dad calls it.

His dad worked forty years in that machine shop and supported a wife and three kids—supported them the best he could which was never good enough for Steve. He wanted more. He wanted to show the old man that he was *somebody!* Now that he *is*—the old buzzard won't comment on it except for that car. He wants that car, Steve thinks. This thought makes him cackle.

His mind is blank for a few minutes as he walks. Not blank but not focused. He contemplates a tree limb that needs the county road commission's attention. He thinks maybe he'll call them about it on Monday. He looks at his running shoes and thinks nothing but shoes, white, shoes, walk. He checks his watch for the time. He thinks about his hemorrhoids and wonders if running will aggravate them—if he ever gets to running again.

There she is. Right there in his head. Someone he'd prefer not to think about and doesn't much any more. Pretty Cindy. She isn't any great beauty but he still thinks of her as his pretty Cindy. Most people would think she's not half as pretty as Joan. It's the sparkle in her eyes more than anything. Steve didn't see the sparkle at first. Cindy informed him, "That's because the sparkle wasn't there when you first met me." She told him that the sparkle came from knowing him. Cindy was the only woman he'd ever remembered really opening up to. He may have opened up to some others but he was drunk, out of town and never saw them again after one night—so they didn't count.

Just thinking about Cindy makes him smile and feel contented. Steve had found Cindy as fascinating as her paintings. She was very straight forward and she had appeared quite confident. As he talked with her at successive meetings, he'd found her layered—like the way she dressed when he first met her. Underneath she was naive and fragile, like Joan had seemed in college, only softer, more complicated, deeper and difficult to soothe.

Cindy had never done a commissioned portrait before. Usually she places her paintings in galleries. Because Steve was her first commissioned portrait she had said that she wanted to spend some time getting to know her subject. Later that was a source of great amusement out at The Tidy View. He'd asked her often if she thought she knew him well enough and she would always say, "Not yet," as she twirled his chest hairs with her finger. Then they'd resume their familiarization process. (Steve jokingly *forbid* Cindy to do another commissioned portrait.)

Before the *familiarization* process, she had taken photographs of his face. Many photographs from different angles. After that she'd come around about once a week to give him a progress report and to *study* him. She had no intention of doing a traditional portrait. He'd understood that from the first. She had said she wanted to try to capture the inner man in her style. Steve had told her he appreciated her creativity and he wasn't concerned with the likeness. He wanted a work of art coincidental to his image being in it. He had offered sincerely, *"I believe in you."* In Cindy's mind, he couldn't have said anything more seductive. She'd been waiting all of her life to hear someone declare, "I believe in you."

About three weeks after he'd given her the deposit, Cindy was sitting with Steve in the conference area in his office. For some reason, Steve had closed the door behind Cindy when she came in. He'd never done that when she'd come before.

Steve was jabbering away about the technical aspects of color printing since she'd expressed interest in offset lithographs of her work. Abruptly Cindy had hid her face in the palms of her hands. Her head had fallen forward. An alarmed Steve had asked, "Are . . . are you okay?" After a few seconds her fingers had slid down her face revealing her eyes first. They'd penetrated Steve. Steve's eyes had locked into hers. She'd lowered both of her hands and had spoken, softly, *"I'm sorry! It's just that I feel so vulnerable when I'm near you."*

Steve had felt the blood in his head do something. He wasn't sure if it was draining or flooding. He couldn't move. He'd never been caught so off guard. He had responded gently from his subconscious which had hoped for something like this. "I feel vulnerable, too."

"I know you're married, Steve," Cindy had said, looking deeply into his eyes. "What is your marriage like?"

Steve's hand was holding his head. His arm was propped up at the elbow by the arm of his chair. He'd answered, "It could be better." He'd thought he sounded mechanical, the way he'd answered so quickly and without any inflection. He'd added, "Okay, but *not good.*" He said it again, "Not good."

He saw a tear roll out a corner of Cindy's right eye as she'd said, "What am I supposed to do about this? Suppress it? Act on it? Pretend it isn't so? This has never happened to me before. I don't know what to do!"

Steve was the one to break the statue pose in which they were both stuck. He'd reached forward and held out his hand. She'd taken it and in the next few weeks, they confessed *everything* to each other. Things Joan didn't know. Of his first love in high school, a teacher fresh out of college whom he kissed in her room after school. Of flunking out of college before Vietnam. Of a Vietnamese woman named Ling, whom he thinks gave birth to his child and about the guilt he feels when he lets himself think about it, wondering what happened to them. He'd told her how when he was first struggling with the business he'd messed with the books, heavily for three years, living in fear that it would be discovered.

Cindy had revealed her lonely childhood. The summer her grandma was visiting and died next to her in bed, and how for years Cindy wondered if she somehow killed her because she disliked her so. She'd told him where her secret pantry of food is located revealing her obsession with chocolate. She'd laid herself open when she spewed out her deepest fear that she's a loser, a dreamer and a loser, who will live and die without meaningful acknowledgment that she'd been here. There were the nightmares of animals being tortured which she'd shared with others, even Bruce. But she whispered to Steve something she'd never told anyone. It was Bruce who in those dreams was stuffing newspaper into the animals mouths, hanging them by their hind legs from ropes, and setting them on fire.

Steve had thought for a while there that he was going to leave Joan for Cindy but when it came right down to it, it was a matter of simple economics—that and the fact that Cindy scared the hell out of him. She was a wild card. She was just beginning to discover herself. Jesus, he and Joan have known themselves for years. Joan's a good looking bitch and he's a hell-of-a-nice-guy and real well-to-do to boot. He cackles again.

Yeah, it was basic economics. Steve sighs as he recalls the moment he realized that he was going back to *life as usual.* The let-down. No more lying in bed with Cindy. The simultaneous relief. No more lying to Joan. Starr's got college coming up—probably more than twenty thousand dollars a year, if she gets in where Joan's planning to send her, and there may be private high school before that. Steve worked his way through college. Nothing came easy for Steven James Gillette, Jr. He earned it all, and he didn't go to elite schools. He went to state schools to get to where he is now. He plain worked hard and simply hustled his butt and brain.

Steve's getting chilled. He's not working up much body heat ambling along the road like this and it's cold out here. He decides to turn around and head back. Before he gets to the driveway, he starts limping.

As he limps across the kitchen Joan says, "That artist who did your portrait telephoned. Mrs. Mead."

Steve maintains his cool as he pours coffee. He doesn't blink or flinch or alter his course. He learned how to maintain composure because of the business. He learned how to play roles there. Hell, he could be a star in any one of those productions of Joan's. "Oh yeah?" he says walking jauntily over to the table.

"For a minute there I thought you were limping. Why are you back so soon?"

"I *was* limping. I *am* limping. I think I pulled something." Steve rubs the back of his thigh.

"You didn't warm up—did you? You shot yourself out that door and down the road. I don't know what you expected. Everybody knows you have to warm up."

Steve freely entertains the idea that if she says one more thing, he might scald her. His psyche is itching to do it. Joan anguishes, *when* did she begin to feel so compelled to belittle him like a condescending, critical parent? But her mind vaults and does a somersault landing squarely on *when* did *he* start acting like a spoiled child? And, when did he start looking so . . . she searches for the words as she looks over at his thinning, gray, oily hair, face stubbled with day old barbs and years and years of impacted pores, and that, that *hat*. He actually went out to jog in that hat. And, then she found the word: nerd! Steve, her handsome, successful husband—she used to gloat about her catch. He looks like someone else's old nerd of a husband. Steve slurps some coffee. If he slurps again Joan fears she may go over the edge. *The butcher knife.* It's part of a set given to them as a wedding present all of those years ago. *The butcher knife.* It glistens conveniently near her right hand. If he slurps again, pacifist or not, she may go for it. *The butcher knife.*

"What did she say—*the artist?*" Steve asks while he puts a slice of raisin bread in the toaster. He hands the line to her like it's a "throw-away" line. Joan taught him that's what they call it in the theater. Inside, he's bracing himself. Steve always refers to Cindy as *the artist* whenever she comes up in conversation with Joan. Before the painting was completed, Joan would query about the progress and refer to *Mrs. Mead.* That's what *she* always calls her, since Joan has never met Cindy. Steve encouraged Joan's vision of her as an eccentric, older woman from the Civic Art Association. Joan had only seen the paintings in that gallery in Ann Arbor. She thought they were not only inferior art but terribly peculiar, like something done for therapy by a mental patient.

The portrait project had dragged on (in Joan's opinion) for six months. Every now and then Joan would ask when Mrs. Mead was planning to finish the portrait that Steve had commissioned for his lobby. One time, Steve had responded, "The artist says it's coming along but she wants me to get my money's worth and she's real fussy about her work. She has very high standards. Who knows, she may be famous someday and I may be hanging in the Metropolitan in New York?" Joan had guffawed at that. She'd been there many times, she had reminded Steve. She couldn't imagine it. "A painter from Reedville?" she'd sneered to Steve. "You and that painter from Reedville in the Metropolitan?" Steve decided right then that before the end of the week he was going to fly Cindy to New York with him. They *would* be in the Metropolitan Museum of Art *together*—and they were for one day last May.

When Joan had finally seen the painting in the lobby outside Steve's office, she knew she was right about it—too *something*. She couldn't explain it. It was too *something* to be considered good. No one liked it. But they didn't like it because *they're* conservative, narrow-minded about art. That's not why Joan didn't like it. She couldn't exactly tell you *why* she didn't like it, other than, it isn't good art, that's all! She's seen enough art, taken enough art appreciation to know. The employees know who's boss, Joan realizes, so they wouldn't dare say they didn't like the painting. His business associates are rarely straight with him about things they know he's sold on. No one would come right out and say they hated it—not even Joan would express it. She feels her opinion doesn't count anyway, when it comes to anything even close to that business. She's never been asked about anything regarding the business or the building—even things she knows about like the aesthetics of landscaping or choosing carpeting or how to entertain out-of-town clients or how to choose real *Art*.

Steve loves that monstrosity. He's obviously blinded by something—egomania—probably. He'd paid the artist three thousand dollars for it. The way Steve feels about money, he'd have to love it and, of course, it was his image—all the more reason he covets it in Joan's opinion. And covet it he did. He still does, *obnoxiously*, Joan feels. He practically genuflects every time he goes by. That's what Edith, his secretary, confided to Joan. Edith has to sit under that thing every day and she's not happy about it. It's the first sight one sees when coming in the front door. Pathetically the first impression of the business. It smacks Joan in the face every time—even when she's prepared and braced for the assault on her sense of aesthetics.

"She says she wants you to call her as soon as possible. Here's her number." Joan shoves a piece of paper across the breakfast nook table. She turns it around, as though Steve doesn't know that number upside down. Steve was sitting right by the wall phone and Joan was staring. It unnerved him!

"I've got to take a crap," he says as he walks off, taking a few steps before he remembers to limp and add some moans.

Joan hates that crassness. Eric never says things like that—"I've got to take a crap." Eric likes classical music and knows how to dance and has a gorgeous body. He ought to have a great body since he's only twenty-eight. Joan doesn't want to think about that. It was over before it began. It never really began except in her dreams. He was kind to her, a dumpy old lady with whom he shared an office, filled with his scent, and now he's moved to Iowa to study playwriting in some prestigious program out there and that empty-headed Jade-person went with him.

Joan wants to drown herself in the lily pond. That's what she was doing out there earlier. She was thinking that she'd like to die in her pond but not until summer when the vegetation is lush and she has everything weeded. She won't kill herself at Christmas. Starr would never have another good one her whole life.

Deep in her heart Joan believes Steve is leaving her. High and dry in her middle years! She'll get a settlement, but no more culinary workshops in New York every summer and in three years she'll be living alone for the first time in her life after Starr goes off to college.

Starr is getting mouthy and trampy looking. There aren't any boyfriends in her life as far as Joan or anyone knows. Joan's been at the school often to consult with the guidance counselor about Starr's academic future. She's sure Helen Beemer would tell her if there was something wrong with Starr. She would detect it like she detects when something is bothering Joan, which is most of the time. And she'd get Starr to confess it the way she gets Joan to confess, and then she'd ask questions that would attempt to get Starr to work on getting things straightened out in her life.

Starr hates me, Joan thinks. Starr doesn't come right out and say it but she continually makes snide comments like her dad. They're a lot alike—distant . . . from Joan. Joan is always on the outside. Starr ridicules her like Steve and she doesn't know how much more she can take.

Steve sits behind a locked door on the john, flipping through a *National Geographic,* looking for breasts, a habit from adolescence. Shortly he's spanning the world. Not touching down anywhere. He's wondering what Cindy wants and he's pissed that she called the house and identified herself. They said their good-bye. They went through their sweet sorrow and now they should get on with their lives. It has been nearly two months with no communication after winding down for several months with many false endings and passionate re-embraces.

Why stir it all up again? *Okay, so he still has feelings.* He's not dead, not yet, and he's not a *complete* asshole. Okay, so he dialed her this morning before she called him—but *he* hung up.

He wants them both for different reasons. It's so complex. And, there's Starr in the middle. If he left he'd lose his shining Starr. She'd not want to see him—she'd slam the door on him. She's like that. She's decisive and everything is either "in" or "out" with Starr. If he left he'd lose her report cards that he gloats over, dramatically. He'd lose her endless prattling at the dinner table. He'd lose her bitching about Romeo's litter box. He'd lose prom night and her first date and . . . everything.

"Whoever said life was easy?" he queries some tribal man with an assortment of objects piercing his face and body. Symbolic. That's how Steve feels—symbolically pierced by that phone call. He drops the magazine and puts his head in his hands. He wants them all and there's no way. The door is locked. He feels safe to let some of it go. Tears drip off his nose landing on the brown man. Steve wonders if that guy ever cries.

"Hey, dad," Starr hollers through the door, startling Steve, "hard shit?"

Steve can't help but chuckle. "Yes, Starr, dearest," he yells out, feigning annoyance—quietly mouthing to the guy from Africa, *"Hard shit!"*

Six

Here I sit, waiting for him . . . again, Cindy laments while sipping Pineapple/Orange juice in carbonated water. Cindy needs stimulation. She's dragging this morning. She's been on the fruit drink diet for a week and lost two pounds. One more to go. She watches that scale like a hawk. Up two, down two! Up three, down three. As Bruce is constantly reminding her, she doesn't want to get fat.

Bruce's chain saw buzzes somewhere down the hill. How many times she waited to hear from Steve—waited for him to return her call—waited for him to get to the motel. He *is* a very busy man. Cindy knows you can't create a business and keep it successful without giving it a great deal of attention. Still, she wanted more. She put so many things on hold, waiting to see what would happen. He had her wrapped around his little finger and she loved it because when he finally did show up or call, he made her feel so important, so valued.

Maybe he won't call. Is it possible that he won't call this time? He said good-bye. They both said it. They both understood and agreed. But Cindy is being tortured by this separation. She can't let go. She feels like she's in a big, dark box, trying to get out. Steve had hold of her hand. He was helping her lift herself out, steadying her while she climbed. Now he's let her go and she's sliding down, down. Cindy is so afraid that she'll never get out. The walls of the box are crushing in around her. She fears that some part of her own psychological makeup may try to slap a lid on it, capturing her inside forever. "Please call me," she says with her eyes closed and hands clasped like she is praying. Instead she is trying to send a telepathic message northwest, even though she doesn't believe in that either

Cindy tries to imagine what it's like in that big, beautiful house. Where are the phones? What kind of bath soap do they use? What do they talk about at breakfast? She's only seen the house from the outside about a thousand times. Every time she goes to town she drives by. Sometimes she leaves the house saying she's going to the store and then she drives by and comes home with a twelve pack of pop. She joked with Steve that maybe he and Joan could adopt her, like a foster wife and she could live in the manor with them. "Hardy har," he'd said, dryly, as he backed her toward the bed. "Would Bruce come, too? So Joan could have a playmate?"

She's seen Joan several times from a distance at the college when she walked down the theater department halls—cruising for a glimpse. When she got one she'd feel like she was going to pass out. She'd recognized Joan from photographs—the ones on Steve's desk and the ones he brought to show her. She's seen pictures of this woman in a bathing suit shot from the back, aimed up from down low, on a sunny day, so the shadows were harsh. Steve took it and pointed out her flaws to Cindy, who couldn't see very many, even though she desperately wished to.

Cindy needs a diet pop. She needs caffeine for stimulation— fruit juice isn't getting it. When she opens the refrigerator, she sees Bruce's beer. Hell, it's not stimulation she decides she needs. Cindy grabs a bottle and pours herself some frothy sedation into a tall ceramic mug.

Cindy's been sneak eating food for years and years. She knows all of the tricks. She has a secret stash in her studio— a private pantry including boxes of chocolate cake mix. She has sat at the table with Bruce sipping a mug filled with cake batter made into a drinkable liquid—passing it off as sugar-free hot chocolate.

Cindy wouldn't want Bruce to catch her with a beer at eleven-thirty in the morning because he doesn't approve of snacking between meals or eating meals at odd hours, let alone drinking alcohol at eleven-thirty. Breakfast, according to Bruce, is to be eaten right after you get up and you are to get up at a decent hour and go to bed at a decent hour, which Cindy doesn't do. She's a night owl. Lunch is to be eaten between noon and one according to Bruce. The evening meal is to be eaten between six and six thirty-seven is stretching it—and there are to be three things to put on your plate which Bruce eats one at a time. First it's the green vegetable. Then it's the lighter of the two main foods. Then it's the other soy-sauced thing. And, since he's developed a sweet tooth, they have *two* chocolate chip cookies at the end while Bruce has coffee. He counts the cookies. He knows when one is missing. That's why Cindy has her own cookies hidden in the studio. She eats the two cookies Bruce doles out and then she eats the package that she has hidden. It's not likely that Cindy, with a beer at eleven-thirty in the morning, would be understood.

Cindy really blew Bruce's mind when she started having a cola after her orange juice every morning. Cindy never drank coffee. "What's the difference between pop and coffee?" she asked. "We're both after the caffeine. Neither have nutritional value and rot your gut. So what's the difference?" He still looked askance at her and said that he drinks coffee for the *taste* and how can she stand to have pop in the morning. Bruce has had one cola a day for the twenty years Cindy's known him.

She doesn't hear the chain saw anymore. Cindy looks out the window and sees Bruce in the woods splitting logs with a wedge and a mallet. She knows exactly how he does it. She helped him for a few years in the beginning. Bruce creates a crack in the log while still holding onto the steel wedge. He taps it gently with a steel mallet until he doesn't have to hold the sharp steel-edged wedge any longer. It stands upright, unsupported by Bruce, in the end of the log, ready to be walloped. He steps back about three feet, raises the mallet over his head and with all his might brings it down on the wedge, forcing a big split. He's a good guy. He really is, she thinks. Look at how hard he's working out there to keep them warm and save some money so they can eat out every Friday. She could never say that Bruce had been bad to her, all he'd ever been is Brucey, her Brucey-goosey. Now, she can't stand him.

Cindy's a cheap drunk. This beer will make her feel high. She'll be a quarter of the way into it by the time she starts to feel relaxed. She's all tensed up and feeling needy. She needs to talk to Steve. She needs to feel his chest. She needs to put the palm of her hand on the back of his neck. She needs a trip to Paris. Cindy hums that World War I song, "How they gonna keep 'em down on the farm after they've seen Paree." Cindy is in agony.

Christmas is around the corner. She's not dragging out all of that stuff to prop and drape and tie it here and there and then two weeks later unprop, undrape, untie and put it all away. The whole thing is such a waste of time but, Bruce expects it. He actually gets cheery at Christmas. He borders on depression fifty weeks of the year and then at Christmas—he's Mr. Cheerful for two weeks.

Cindy goes back to wondering what's going on at Steve's house. She's seen pictures of the inside. It's spacious and their furniture looks expensive. Cindy got hers at Goodwill. It would have been foolish to buy good furniture with all of the cats and dogs they had at one time. Besides, furniture is on Cindy's want list not Bruce's. For several years Cindy barely made enough to make her truck payment, pay her six months of the electric bill, her share of the property taxes, the phone bill and buy her personal products. For years she even had to borrow money from Bruce who kept a tally. She didn't mind not having nice furniture. She chose to help animals by giving them a home and food and vet care. Bruce chose to help her by giving her a home and food and medical insurance. She was truly grateful when Bruce lovingly suggested, "Let's get married," adding, endearingly at the time, "I always have leftovers."

Joan has it all, including weekly housekeeping services with laundry—every woman's dream. She's got it. The *Citizen-Times* featured the house once. Specifically they featured the Polynesian theme deck and hot tub area in a full page article entitled, "Luxury Decks For Entertainment and Relaxation." There was a photograph of Starr in the hot tub, sipping through a straw from a glass that had a lemon or lime wedge on the rim and a sprig of some leafy thing. Steve told Cindy that the photographer from the *Citizen-Times,* some "punk journalism intern" from Michigan State University, as Steve described him, wanted to photograph Starr reclining sexily beside the hot tub and Starr was all for it. She had on that little two piece thing that barely covers her behind, Steve explained.

"Things are changing at the house," Steve told Cindy the day after the photograph was taken. He and Joan had to put their foot down and overrule Starr on that pose. In the past, they'd been able to reason with Starr—let her make the *right* decision through a *democratic* process. But their agreeable little Starr had revolted and after the intern photographer left, Steve said it was as though someone had unleashed a mad dog. Starr had stomped around the deck, ranting about being embarrassed by her parents and it's her life and she's proud of her body and they can't tell her what to do. The only thing she didn't do, Steve said, was froth at the mouth and bite them.

Steve had said that Joan was totally traumatized by the tirade. She'd called her therapist for a special family session. She'd wanted the therapist to handle this except

97

Elaine was out of town attending a conference about treating adolescents with conduct disorders. Joan had covered the mouthpiece of the phone and asked Steve if this was an *emergency* because if this was, they could see another therapist in the practice.

Steve had told Cindy that he'd responded with, "Jeez, Joan, do you have to ask me about everything?" So Joan had hung up, he said, and had gone to bed right then at four in the afternoon. Steve had said she looked comatose until the alarm went off the next morning. When she came into the kitchen for breakfast Joan acted as though nothing had happened the afternoon before even though a front window had a sheet of plywood nailed to it. She *must* have heard the shattering glass (which Steve cleaned up) and the hammering afterward.

According to Steve, this is how the window was shattered. After Joan had retreated to bed, at four in the afternoon. Steve said he sat on a deck chair and watched Starr until she wound down from her tirade. He didn't know what else to do. She'd stomped to her room slamming the door behind her. But not until after Starr had pulled one of Steve's golf clubs from his bag which was propped by the sliding glass doors. On her way through the dining room Starr had used one of Joan's crystal glasses as a tee and then had hurled the club through one of the big front windows. Steve said he'd got this sharp pain in his chest that ran down his arm and left it numb for several hours.

The largest photograph in the article about the deck covered a quarter of the page. It was Joan in a crisp, obviously linen dress with three flounces at the bottom. Joan wouldn't be wearing that skirt and blouse, Cindy believes, if Joan had to wash and iron it. Joan was smiling, looking like a middle-aged sorority sister, sitting at a low wooden table with plump pillows for seats. The table was set for a luncheon with glass plates that looked like watermelon slices with, according to the article, fused-glass seeds.

Millicent Gordon, the Lifestyle writer at the *Citizen-Times*, described everything with great embellishment—the plates, the flowers, the statues, the lily pond, the nature trail, the imported fabric on the cushions, the Tahitian punch recipe which Joan *improvised* from a recipe that appeared in the July/August issue of *Career Woman on the GO*.

Every time Cindy reads that article she blows a raspberry directly at Joan's face. Cindy would like to see what Millicent would say about her humble little home.

> The hillside home of Mr. and Mrs. Bruce Mead is perched high on a lovely, wooded hill overlooking the Spurr's go-cart track below. Chicken wire kennels and cages in various stages of rust and decay dot the natural yard which hasn't been mowed in three weeks and is up to one's calf, which doesn't bother Mr. Mead because he's "got a mower that can handle it." The centerpiece of the Kennel Collection is the five foot high chain link fence that rises majestically out of the middle of the yard. Mr. Mead states, "We put it there because the soil in that spot is almost pure sand and I figured we'd never get anything to grow there." According to Mr. Mead the whole yard has been struggling for twenty years to turn green. "Grass don't grow in gravel," commented neighbor, Mike Spurr when he came over during the interview to borrow the post hole diggers that it turned out he'd never returned.
>
> Mrs. Mead employs a nostalgic theme in her house to create a homey atmosphere. It's the mountain home "hillbilly" look. The theme is repeated through furniture, appointments, and clever decorative touches that only an

artist would imagine—clothes on a clothesline across the living room, vintage furniture from the nineteen-seventies and eighties (many found in a quaint, junk shop over by the sewage plant), dust balls as big as tumble weeds and intricately woven cobwebs which Mrs. Mead carefully vacuums around. As we sat together at the lovely electrical spool table (circa 1972), Mrs. Mead served this reporter a lovely drink of chocolate cake batter which was so thick we ate it with a Kroger's giveaway spoon.

Cindy would love to see what Millicent would write about this place. *Maybe* she would focus on the good stuff. There's plenty of it here. Peaceful days and quiet nights where the most annoying disturbance is in the spring when horny frogs get to thumping all night in the water-filled low spot. The sun absolutely *pours* in through the windows on the south like honey from a jug. And the woods explodes in the spring with white trillium while the ferns unfurl before your eyes. People stop on the road mesmerized as mother nature throws open her windows and rolls out her lush flora carpet!

When the house was loaded with critters, one was always greeted with a welcoming ballet performed by beings who thought Cindy and Bruce were the greatest beings who ever lived (except for themselves, of course). These are the beings who dive into paper bags and leap from tall countertops much to one's amusement. Competing for applause were the whining tap dancers. Everyone was working themselves into a frenzy, punctuated with occasional snaps or swats, that expressed frustration over having to share the spotlight Cindy and Bruce shone on them.

You'll never get yelled at in Cindy's house for not using a coaster. You'll never get scolded for dropping popcorn on the sofa. The slipcover is washable and replaceable from the Sears catalogue. You never have to worry that you're going to break a glass. The Marathon station is always giving them away.

But just as Cindy's dwelling can sound pretty dreary when it isn't completely, Steve's house, which sounds wonderful in the paper, can be viewed less favorably. Steve and Joan have a Great Room in which no one in the family is allowed unless they have important guests. It's white—floor to ceiling. Even when they have guests Joan's on edge all evening worrying about their "white stuff."

They have a yard that the lawn service people must mow in certain patterns because Joan needs the patterns to follow the contours of the yard. She insists that the carpet in the great room bear no crush marks from the vacuum or feet. The community would never have guessed, looking at the photo of a beaming Joan, that Starr was in the background mumbling obscene words in a nasty little voice and working herself up enough to put a golf club through the front window.

The smallest photograph on the front page of Section C that day was in the lower right hand corner. If you looked closely, you would recognize Steve in a hammock, surrounded by low-growing flowers and bushes in pots along with what Cindy thought were cement gargoyle-type statuary that must be Polynesian.

That article really got to Cindy. Last summer Cindy finally began to realize that she didn't want to keep it up forever—that she wanted more while she feared that Steve liked things the way they were—or maybe even wanted out. That article made her insanely jealous. She still has it. She used to stare at the pictures and imagine life at Steve and Joan's. Then she'd imagine life at Steve and Joan's with herself playing the part of Joan—conveniently eliminating the character named Starr.

She would imagine Steve and Joan in the evening—Joan in a rose colored negligee with black lace and Steve in silk pajamas. Earlier Joan had taken a leisurely scented herbal oil bath while sipping on white wine in a tall smoky goblet. Steve shaved, showered and splashed on the French cologne that his darling Joan gave him for Christmas last year along with a beautiful silk pajama and robe set from Hudson's and three romantic Jazz CD's. They meet out on the deck, under the moon and stars, where there are no mosquitoes. Silk clothing slips off their shoulders and falls to their ankles at the same second. They *gracefully* recline together in the hammock, a real trick for the rest of the world; for them it's easy. Steve pulls her face to his and they kiss *deeply and passionately.* They leave the hammock swinging behind them as he leads her to the hot tub like she's a virgin about to purify a whole civilization of heathens. Oh jeez, they're . . . not *purifying* and that Joan—she's no virgin.

Or . . . She could see Joan in a short cotton night shirt, long-legged, padding barefoot down to the entertainment room and plopping down on the sofa next to Steve while he's reading some business papers with the TV tuned to some "infotainment" show that doesn't require much attention. "Hi, guy," she says as she fingers his shirt collar. Steve looks up from his papers, smiles and says to Joan, "How's my lady-love?" Cindy feels like puking. Of course when she imagines it again and it's *her* with Joan's long legs and he says that to *her,* she melts in his arms.

Or . . . Madam Cindy looks into the crystal ball in her head and finds the scenario of Joan and Steve that she likes the best. She's in this one playing herself.

Steve's in the kitchen getting a bowl of bedtime cereal and Joan marches in with black circles under her eyes from smeared mascara and says, "I want a divorce, asshole!"

Steve says, with his mouth full of cereal, "When? Tomorrow?"

And she says, "My lawyer will call yours, fuckface."

"That's fine with me!" Steve yells at her. "He can call my lawyer 'fuckface' anytime he wants."

"SHE," Joan says. "SHE will call your lawyer, fuckface." She storms out, furious as hell.

"Bitch!" he hollers after her. "Fuuuucking Biiiiitch!" Steve mumbles, "She didn't even get it—that fuckface shit!" Steve puts on his jacket, grabs his car keys and leaves for the Holiday Inn. He calls Cindy from his car phone and tells her to go there immediately. "We're in a whole new ball game," Steve says and adds, "I love ya, babe! I need ya!" Cindy is speechless! *The Holiday Inn is right downtown.* Cindy can finally walk into a decent place holding her head high. She's going to be *legitimate.* She's in love and she's getting her guy and she's *not* going to feel guilty about *nothin'*—except maybe Bruce. "Come as soon as you can," he says, adding, "but try to disguise yourself. And don't walk up and talk to me in the lobby, just follow me to my room, at a safe distance. *This could be messy."* Unfortunately, directed day dreams sometimes veer off the script and develop a life of their own.

Do Joan and Steve argue all of the time? Do they wander that big house rarely running into each other and when they do, are they simply polite? Cindy can't quite capture the tone of life in that house except to know that beneath their best intentions, disillusionment festers and loneliness grows slowly like a blue-green mold on stale bread. Cindy believes there is a deep connection to Joan that Steve won't acknowledge. She understands that connection because she feels it for Bruce. It's based on an intimate knowledge of who this person is *or was.* It's about history. They knew me *when.* It's about a commitment that was *sincerely* entered into. It's about knowing someone well, maybe too well.

How often does Steve take Joan in his arms and . . . it could drive Cindy crazy thinking about it and it could drive her crazy waiting to hear from him. She really needs to talk him into seeing her. Cindy needs to confess her feelings, mourn the loss of her lover with her confessor, who happens to be her ex-lover Steve.

The chain saw starts up again. "Oh well," she says with a resigned sigh. Cindy taps her fingers on the table. She will write that story. She will tell *The True Story of Jimmy Trueberry*—the one he outlined for her when he came back Friday. The kid's life is so pitiful that it made Cindy want to cry. In fact she did do a lot of sniffling making Jimmy nervous.

Cindy saw right away that the story has a lot of the elements of a good book, like death, betrayal, love, hate, almost a double murder with suicide, although a completed double murder with suicide would have been better. "Almost a murder" is like Oprah's always saying about stuff. "That's like being a little pregnant. Either you are or you aren't."

Cindy writes at the top of a new notebook on the first page: *Dack Dick's Novel.* Her pen does some hash marks across the paper. Cindy's thinking. Her pen twirls and zags. Cindy's still thinking. Her pen adds another *Novel* after the first. Cindy looks at it. *Dack Dick's Novel Novel.* Cindy is amused. She scratches out the last *Novel*, looks at it for a minute and writes *Navel.* She finds herself contemplating *Dack Dick's Novel Navel.* Ha! There it is! God, what a wit! Cindy giggles before she scratches the whole line out. She's ready to begin. *The True Story of Dack Dick.*

> *Dack Dick wanders aimlessly across the freshly plowed fields of the farmer he'd about killed, like a human herbicide eradicating the weeds of his life. If Dack had completed what he'd gone back there to the shack to do this murderous May night, his*

mother would lay dead beneath the big man's body—a body much like his own, sun-browned, chiseled, well-meated.

Cindy reads over what she has written, tears the paper off, wads it up and throws it on the table. Jimmy wouldn't understand poetic license. He'd think he looks like that. She thinks again before she begins to write:

> *It was a cold, snowy day, typical for Michigan at that time of year when a young man named Dack Dick plowed his way up the driveway to push Deidre's doorbell. It was ten o'clock and Deidre was still sipping expresso at the round, antique oak table in the dining room of her Victorian home. She had mailed her latest novel to New York City to her editor, Lauren Levant-Roepke. This last book had been her most challenging, and Deidre was relieved to be taking her time to start a new day. The last few weeks had been such a strain. Deidre is allergic to deadlines.*

> *She didn't have the foggiest idea of what she would write next until a crestfallen, young man named Dack rang her bell. Ring!*

The phone rings. It startled Cindy who jumped up from her spool table to see if she would see Bruce out the window. He is coming up the hill on his tractor. She grabs the wall phone in the kitchen. "Hello?" she says as a question.

"Hi, ya!" Steve says, cheerfully and, then *whispers*, "I assume it's safe to talk?" as though someone standing near Cindy might hear the first part but not the last.

"Yes, for just a minute," she says.

105

He snaps, "Whadaya want?" Cindy might cry . . . later. She's so happy to hear his voice that she doesn't care what he says to her or how he says it.

"Steve, I need to see you! Just one more time. I need to get some things settled in my mind. Can we get together? Not at The Tidy View. I don't mean that. Just to talk." There is silence on the other end. "Steve," she says, "I can't talk very long, Bruce is on his way in! Can't we get together one more time?"

Steve's holding his head. His eyes are closed. Joan's gone to the store and taken Starr. He doesn't know what to say. Maybe he owes it to her but maybe it's a trap. She may want to pound him with her purse like Joan did with the pillow. What's the point, he thinks. "What's the point?" he asks.

"The point is," Cindy starts to say until she hears Bruce coming in the door. "Damn! Bruce is coming! Call me tomorrow during the day." She hangs up.

Bruce is sweating under his plaid, wool jacket. Sweat runs down his forehead. He pulls his knit cap off. His salt and pepper hair is soaking wet. He moans as he plops into a chair at the table. Cindy turns her back and goes down to the studio with her notebook and wadded-up rejects. She sits at her drawing table. She stares out the window which Jack Frost has beautifully etched. Another winter, she thinks. Another Christmas. One life. She starts to write.

> We are all alone. We are all together. Bonded as strangers walking blindly through darkness to the end of our story. A being is born without knowledge that he or she may die too soon, carried away as easily as dust rides the rain or spared as precariously as air floats wings. And there is nothing to be done to stop the sun from setting on one's day . . . as it rises on another's.

Cindy holds up the tablet and reads what she wrote. She reads it again. Her hands drop to the table. She reads it out loud, " . . . *as easily as dust rides the rain or spared as precariously as air floats wings. And there's nothing to be done to stop the sun from setting on one's day as it rises on another's.*" It gives her the willies—all of the symbolism and meaning and so poetic in sound and imagery. Did she actually write this? Cynthia Wickett Mead? How did she do it? My god, Cindy thinks, look at all of the stuff I thought of to describe my work. It's like she might understand something about writing or at least *her* writing.

She wants to fall to her knees. Is this a religious experience, Cindy wonders, through a rush of excitement? Whatever it is, it is short-lived because when Cindy looks at her writing again, a few seconds later, "*. . . as easily as dust rides the rain.*" Oh, god, *she loathes it!* Does air float wings? For a fraction of a second, though, she thinks maybe she likes it again. No—no! She doesn't and so she wads up that page and throws it away, too. Actually, she burns it in her heat stove in the studio. There's no reason to leave any evidence around of this thing she's doing.

The pen goes back down on the paper, but she doesn't write anything. As the ink soaks into the yellow legal pad in an ever-enlarging black circle, all kinds of thoughts flit around inside Cindy's head—bouncing like Ping-Pong balls off her brain walls. When her thoughts quiet down, Cindy flips several pages over and calmly writes: *Dear Steve,*

Do you know how I miss you—how often I think of you—how often I wonder what you are doing at that precise moment? There is so much that we will never know of each other's lives and I was hoping that you would be the one to know everything about me. I find myself much of the time wanting to tell you of my thoughts, of what I saw or did. I find it impossibly difficult to accept that if you are in trouble, I will not be there to help. I picture you late at night,

107

alone on your deck looking up to realize that you can't remember how it felt to hold me. You know me well enough to know that I am suffering because I don't let go easily, but Steve . . . I am leaving. Finally letting go of it all. I wanted to say good-bye in person because I am moving away. I wanted to tell you how you changed my life. How grateful I will always be for having known you. You will never hear from me again—unless I hear from you. Love, Cindy.

Cindy's been dropping tears on the paper and several of the words are floating in saline. She'd like to let out the feelings that have knotted up inside. Let them go. Right now! It's all up there, so close to the surface, wanting to escape. Instead, she flips the page, looks at it for a while and writes with a calm coldness: *Dear Bruce,*

As you know, I have been acting—Cindy crosses out "acting" and writes "exhibiting"—As you know, I have been exhibiting signs for over a year that things are not good between us. I am not happy. Over the last five years, I have been changing. I no longer want to live isolated, safely, for an isolated, safe life has come to feel like no life at all.

Cindy is startled by a ring of the phone. Before she gets to the studio extension, it stops ringing. She hears Bruce's footsteps cross the kitchen above her, enter the hall and walk into the bathroom. "Cindy," he yells down the register, "it's for you, some guy."

Seven

A guy calling? Sunday at noon? She just talked to Steve—God love him. He must not be able to wait until tomorrow. It's got to be Steve! Who else would it be? Cindy yells up that she'll get it in the studio. She runs across the room and picks up the receiver. Then she runs back across to the door and yells up the stairwell for Bruce to hang up the phone. Just as she gets back to the phone, she hears Bruce hang up, roughly. And she could swear she heard a big belch in the background just before the receiver hit the cradle. Bruce belches loudly to display displeasure. Cindy used to think they were random belches from that touchy digestive track. Now she knows better. She knows that they're well-placed, despite Bruce's denial. He's always got one ready to shove out when he feels like it. He has gas ready to come out both ends at any given time.

Her heart is pounding! Just what does Steve think he's doing calling her up, knowing that Bruce is in the house? She's not angry. She's actually excited—like when she imagines Steve driving up to her house, charging in and announcing to Bruce that Cindy is going with him, and then driving off with her to a new life where there's an ocean and romance—maybe northern California or Cape Cod.

It's so exciting for him to be so daring, Cindy thinks, suddenly not caring one hoot about the risk. She and Steve play so well together. She is amused as she breaths heavily into the mouthpiece and then in her sexiest purr says, "Howdy, Tiger Stud."

There is a pause before a voice says, "Is this Mrs. Cindy Mead?"

(Who the hell is this?) She's not sure what to do or say. "Who? Who do you want?" Cindy asks, trying to sound calm.

"I want Mrs. Cindy Mead!" the voice says, harshly

"Who is this?" Cindy asks. She feels faint. She might faint.

"Never mind who this is! I want to talk to Mrs. Cindy Mead!"

Cindy pushes her finger down on the hang-up button.

Eugene doesn't realize that he's been hung up on. "Mrs. Mead," he says, "I want ta know what my boy was doing at yer house the other day when he shoulda been in school! Don't try ta deny it. I got it from good connections that his car was in yer driveway. If yer involved in any drug sellin' or prostitution, I'll have yer ass . . . " A dial tone pierces his ear as the caller disconnect function finally kicks in. "Damn Bitch," he says as he slams the receiver down. The old phone table nearly collapses from the force.

Howdy Tiger Stud, he replays. Its got to be prostitution. He'd heard years ago that woman was into nudism. Eugene is no dummy. His mind has it all figured out. But before he says anything to Jimmy or Lizzie Jo, he's going to have this lady's ass in a legal sling. He may even get famous over this. The guys at work will bust a gut. The only problem is that it's his kid's use of her that tipped Eugene off, and even though it's not such a bad thing, really, to use a prostitute, he's not sure he wants his kid on the front page of the *Citizen-Times*. Jesus Christ, *his* picture might even get on the front page coming out of the courtroom or something. Then Princess and her niece might come forward to defend one of their own who has less cooperation from the police and prosecutor who turn a blind eye to Princess's operation. Hell, that doesn't make sense—Cindy Mead would be a competitor of Princess. In that case Princess would be glad to have her put out of business unless this Mead woman is some kind of rural branch of Princess's. He thought Princess had a monopoly on Reed County. Eugene decides he'll have to feel her out while she's tying him up, the next time he's in there. Those bitches might even point their finger at Eugene who's spent some good bucks with Princess over the years. The more he thinks about it, the more he thinks this could get pretty damn sticky. Good thing he's got a sharp enough mind to figure out all the pitfalls. There's not much that gets by me, Eugene thinks.

Eugene decides not to call Cindy back—at least not now. He puts on his jacket and heads out to the barn. Jimmy and Lizzie Jo are both gone. Lizzie went to church and then to see her friend, Doris. Doris Thompson's in a nursing home, *prematurely*. She's only fifty-eight but she's got emphysema real bad. She'll probably die within a year, according to Lizzie. It's just as well, Eugene thinks. All of her life, Doris has been sucking off the taxpayers who'll probably have to *bury* her, too.

Jimmy's off somewhere blowing his summer farm-work money on gasoline for that car. Works like a dog for other farmers for money on top of doing his own chores around here all summer and then he drives all that sweat and muscle-aching work off in that car which he wouldn't have if his Aunt Rose hadn't given it to him when her brat got himself busted for larceny.

Rose and Kink really got theirs with that last kid. They should have quit at three. The first three did pretty good. Sherry's married to a supervisor in some Japanese auto parts plant over in Cherryvale. Being an American supervisor in a slant-eye plant is some hot-shit thing according to Kink. Vale is in the Navy getting electronics training. Melinda's

111

going to the community college to be a nurse. But Travis, he's trouble. At least my kid ain't sittin' in the county tank, Eugene thinks. Will's sitting in his fat aunt and fat granny's kitchen. He probably had homemade cinnamon rolls for breakfast.

Will seemed to have money to burn and nobody knew for sure where he got it. He sure didn't work for it. Will was headed for trouble—big trouble. He'd already been in a lot of little trouble.

Eugene decides he'll change the oil in his truck. It's several hundred miles past time. He drives the truck into the barn.

Eugene and Will were about to come to blows. In fact, they did come to blows. That kid's got a mouth on him that could incite a riot in a beehive in January. If the kid hadn't been faster than Eugene, he'd have had a fireplace poker across his back when he was asked for about the fifth time to get his ass off the couch and feed the goddamn pigs. When Will said, "Why don't you get outa my fuckin' face?" Eugene flipped. He grabbed the first thing he saw that looked lethal but by that time Will was up and running for his car in his stocking feet. Eugene laid that poker across Will's Trans-Am spoiler and cracked it good as Will sped off toward Indiana where he showed up five hours later, shoeless and spoiless.

When Eugene took out after Will that day, Lizzie took out after Eugene. She grabbed Eugene and started pounding on him with her fists. Eugene couldn't believe it. She's always been such a puss—quiet—no spunk. She wasn't no puss that day. He had bruises to prove it. And people are always making such a big deal out of wife abuse. What about him? She couldn't really hurt him, though. He thought it was funny. He was laughing the whole time she was pounding. In fact, she was turning him on.

Eugene sticks a pan under the truck and crawls under to unscrew the plug and filter. He should have married Helga and brought her here. She would have been a good wife. Those German gals knew how to please a man. They cook and clean good and they screw good, Eugene thinks. His life would have been a whole lot better if he'd have asked Helga to marry him—or one of the others. Hell, they were all dying to be an American like everyone else around the world. But, he had some wild-assed notion that he was in love with Lizzie—she had such big tits for such a little thing.

Eugene lays with his back on the straw and watches the oil drain. He can see his breath. *Terry.* He reaches over and turns off the trouble light. It's shining in his eyes. *Terry.* He thinks of Terry. Why does he always have to think of *Terry* when he does this? He couldn't help it. It wasn't his fault. He didn't know they were out there. Terry and Jimmy were playing under the truck. He just didn't know. He was going to town. He can't remember *why* he was going to town. It was a Saturday. Eugene hates weekends. Ever since then, he's hated weekends. Before that November, he lived for them. Now, he prefers being at work. It's predictable there and nobody makes you want to shut them up. He and the guys get along great. They all understand each other. It's the wives and kids that drive you crazy. All the guys feel the same way.

Eugene's dad said that Terry looked just like Eugene when he was a baby. Poor kid! What's he thinking "poor kid"—about the boy looking like himself? That kid never got to be three years old. Now there is something to think "poor kid" about . . . or is it? What's so great about life anyway, Eugene thinks? My ma beat us around and then left when I was ten. So I got to be ten, he thinks. So I got to be ten. Big deal! And now, I'm almost forty. So what? I got one kid run over and one run off and one running around all of the time.

Eugene wonders what it feels like to get run over by a truck. He toys with the idea of finding out. He could rig it up; he could find out. Shit, it would be easy.

She's down there in Florida or so Sis heard. His ma's married for the third time—maybe more by now. She's down there in Florida with the lizards and the palm trees and hurricanes. She's painted her long nails red. That's how Eugene remembers her, with long, red nails, dragging on a cigarette. Maybe she has emphysema, too. Maybe not. Maybe she's making some craggy faced old man (who might be his stepdad) her famous Fudge Divine. She's rolling a ball of it around with her fingernail in the bottom of a cup of cold water to see if it's boiled enough to pour on a buttered dish to let it sit and cool. She'll cut it into squares and pile it onto a clean plate. Eugene wonders, who scrapes the pan? Who licks the spoon? Who makes the mommy happy with his pants down? Does the old lady ever think of that? Does she ever think of that licking the spoon shit? Loving him one minute while she did that and hitting him around the next. What's really funny to Eugene is that he liked it both ways, all at once, and still does.

Jesus Christ, why must he *always* think such crap when he's under the truck changing the oil! Eugene turns the light back on, screws the drain shut and puts on the new filter. He's got a bunch of work to do around here today and he's been laying under the truck thinking about stuff that nobody can do anything about. He ought to be thinking about what to do with Jimmy and that Mead "lady"—an odd choice of a word for a hooker, he thinks.

Eugene chuckles when he thinks of his kid getting it on with a hooker. Kinda funny when he thinks about it. The horny little shit probably gets it off before he gets it in. It's like that when you're that age. They don't give refunds, them girls. He probably pays for *nothin'*.

It's pretty unusual for a prostitute to be working in the country, but come to think of it, he's always wondered why someone would stick a house way up there. The only reason Jimmy's car was seen was because it was only halfway up there—probably like Jimmy when he goes bang. Eugene chuckles again. Still, he thinks those women should stay in town and not be messing around out in the country. People out here are decent. There ain't no country niggers like down south, he thinks. And there ain't supposed to be no country hookers. Whores, yeah. There's whores everywhere—women who do it for free. Hell, it's never completely free. Women always want somethin' Eugene thinks.

Eugene has poured in the oil. He decides he needs to go to the store to get himself some chew. It wouldn't hurt to get that clean oil moving around in there. He turns the ignition key. The engine starts and stalls. The second time, he pumps the petal a little. It cranks and then gets a hold. He races the engine. The bitch that has taken up residence in the old pump house is roused by the racket. She comes out to bark and chase the car out to the road and down it a little. Eugene thinks he's going to have to do something about that dog soon—it's a pain, the way it won't come to you and chases cars. It has been around two weeks. He's told Lizzie not to feed it, but he suspects she does. She probably gave it leftover pancakes from this morning. He hasn't found any dead pigs or barn cats. But it's living off something and Eugene suspects it's living off *him* through his wife's candy-assed sympathy. Women are such pusses. They're always living off a man just like that bitch dog. Eugene decides he's gonna kill that bitch before she pops those pups. Her tits are swinging. He'll have to do it soon—today or tomorrow.

Eugene looks at Jerry Kerry's farm as he goes by. He went to school with Jerry who like Eugene inherited his father's place. Eugene and Jerry were both in Ag classes and Future Farmers of America together. He and Jerry went to some state FFA competition in Grand Rapids when they were seniors. Neither one of them placed. Then they both graduated and Eugene got a job at Wolverine Auto Connection stocking shelves. Eugene got called up but not to Nam where he wanted to go. Jerry went to Michigan State University and came home four years later to take over the farm. He'd gone to Germany during college on some kind of agricultural exchange thing and he didn't even try to look up Eugene. It pissed Eugene off when he heard about it in a letter from Lizzie Jo. She'd read about Jerry's trip in the paper.

Jerry turns out 20,000 hogs a year between his three farms. He's got most of it automated. That farm's run like a factory. He showed Eugene around once. Jerry showed Eugene a room where they run a sow up on what they call the rape rack after giving her an injection to induce the release of the eggs and this super expensive boar takes her until he's done. Then Jerry's workers march in another sow to the tune of a "hot-shot"—jabbing her with some voltage until they can clamp her in the rack. The next stud boar who according to Jerry was bred in Iowa is ushered in to do his thing. He explained about those Iowa boars, but it was hard to understand because it involved test tubes and mother pigs carrying some other pigs special genes. Shit, it was a some story! Eugene wonders if it was all true? It sounds too good to Eugene.

Those sows are put into single pens just big enough for one pig. There are several buildings with these sows standing or laying in cement floor pens growing piglets. Then they are transferred to the farrowing buildings right before they give birth. Jerry had said, "You can't imagine the ruckus in this place when we take their young for sorting, tail docking, castrating and vaccinating. When the sows hear all that squealing, they act like we're killing their young. If they only knew that we treat them like gold because that's what they are to us here at the corporation." Of course Eugene knows that pigs squeal over anything.

Jerry told him the piglets get sorted according to weight. All the ones with the same weight get put together. The sows don't know any difference about which pigs they birthed. Jerry emphasized that vaccinating and regular antibiotics are a necessity in this kind of operation because disease can wipe out a whole building if it gets going. Jerry's got those pigs in buildings from birth to when they load them up for the slaughterhouse. It's really something! Boy, those pigs have got it made—so's Jerry, Eugene thinks.

Makes my eighteen hogs look pretty ridiculous, he figures. He wonders what Jerry thinks when he drives by Eugene's place. Jerry's a nice guy but Eugene knows they haven't got anything in common anymore—even though they both graduated together and they're both raising pigs. Jerry's oldest girl is in Jimmy's class but Jimmy says she's stuck-up and Eugene thinks he's probably right.

Eugene turns on the radio right in the middle of a Tammy Wynette wail. Now there's a woman. Shit, if he could have Tammy Wynette, he'd know he'd died and gone to heaven. Eugene likes the old-time singers better. The new ones are trying too hard to catch on outside of country music, attracting the wrong kind of people. Someday he's going to take Lizzie Jo down to Fan Fare in Nashville; so she can go to the Grand Ol' Opry, meet some of the stars—get their autographs.

Oh shit, Eugene thinks, here comes that song that makes me feel so bad. It's about a man who comes home from work one day to find that his wife of ten years has gone off and left him with the kids. There's just a tear-stained note laying on the table and a little memento for each of the kids to remember her by. It rips Eugene up inside to hear that song. It's by one of the new guys but this one does it old-time country. Eugene has to watch it or he may actually shed a tear over those last two lines: *"And mama loves you all and Daddy too, but I'm on my way to Californeeay. I'm on my way to Californeeay."*

Eugene wipes at the corner of his eye as he rounds the bend by the township cemetery. He cranks his head to the right and looks back in where his dad and Terry are buried. Shit, what do you think he sees? Jimmy's jalopy is parked back in there. Eugene slows down, cranes his neck. He wonders how often Jimmy goes there? Eugene hasn't been there since they stuck Terry in. Lizzie Jo goes over every memorial day and fixes it up with some artificial flowers that she probably pays a fortune for. She probably goes on Terry's birthday and maybe the anniversary, but Eugene has no idea how often she or anybody else goes there. All he knows is he's not going. Lizzie tried to get him to go with her at first until she figured out that *he meant it.* He can't say how many times he had to say "I ain't goin'." Sometimes women just keep it up until you have to grab them and make sure they understand. She hasn't asked for a long time.

Eugene pulls in to Buddy's. He'll get a little gas. When he pulls up to the pump, Sherman Miller comes out the door. "Hey Gene!" he yells over. He's unwrapping a pack of cigarettes as he walks toward Eugene. "Where you been keepin' yourself? I ain't seen you in a while!" he yells.

Eugene despises Sherman Miller. He's hated him all his life and Sherman's always been so friendly. Eugene nods an acknowledgment at Sherm, hoping he will keep on walking. Just as Eugene gets the nozzle into his tank opening, here comes Sherm right up to him and says, "I just saw Spike Williams over at the Red Dog last night. Ain't that a coincidence? And we was sayin', 'wonder what Gene's up to?' Spike's on disability. He fell off a scaffolding on his job and cracked-up his back real good. It's been kinda hard 'cause his wife left him a couple of years ago and he's not got nobody to help him out. I'm thinkin' maybe the Grange could do a fund-raiser 'cause even though he's got that disability check and all, he's got a lot of bills that he cain't get paid."

In high school Spike wouldn't have anything to do with Sherman or himself once he got on the basketball team. Now that he's hard up he'll sit next to Sherm at the bar and act like they were always friends. Sherm's a fool, Eugene thinks as he shuts the nozzle off at five dollars and six cents. Sherm made him shoot over his target by six cents. That's the kind of thing he hates Sherm for. Eugene screws the gas cap back on, slaps the little door shut and walks away from Sherm without saying a word but Sherm trails after him lighting one of those cigarettes and says, "Like when he first got hurt, he had to hire a nurse to come in every day to make him a meal and help him take a bath and shave him and all. That wasn't covered. I guess they figured . . . " Eugene walks in the door to pay but because Sherm's smoking, he stays out and looks across the road, waiting for Eugene to come back. Eugene asks for his tobacco and then wanders the mini-mart hoping Sherman Miller will get in his car and leave. But it's too much to ask. Finally Eugene grabs a pop and a bag of ranch-flavored somethings and goes up to pay for it all.

When he goes out the door he sees that Sherm has cornered Lonnie Pitman over at the air hose. Sherm's back is to Eugene who walks to his truck and starts to drive away. Sherm waves at him as he pulls out and yells, "Nice to see ya, Gene! Keep yer wig warm!"

That guy's a pussy, Eugene thinks. Now, there's a real pussy-man. If he's seen Sherm cry once he's seen it a hundred times. Anything could set Sherm off. He'd cry if he didn't get chosen for a team—which he rarely did. He'd cry if you looked like you were going to hit him—which you always did. He'd cry when a horse fell in a movie. He cried like the girls when Kennedy got shot. He'd cry when he lost his dad's fountain pen (which Eugene had taken). He'd cry at anything. All the guys hated him. They all figured it was because he was adopted. Sherman, Sr. and Bertha were older when they got Sherm and they turned him into a wimp, fawning over him like he was the second Jesus Christ when he was more than likely some teenage girl's bastard.

Eugene went over there when he was a kid for Shermy's birthday party or some other twinkie thing. They were scrambling for friends for him even then. Eugene didn't know these people until they picked him off the road when he was propelling dirt clods at passing cars. He'd missed his target when the target suddenly stopped and backed up. Eugene wasn't afraid. He figured he could outrun anybody from the same starting place.

Bertha, Shermy's ma had stuck her head out the window and yelled, "Come over here, honey, I want to ask you something." She'd asked him how old he was and after he said "Six," she asked if he'd like to go to a birthday party? He was ready to drop his next dirt bomb and get in the car right then. He wasn't sure about Shermy who sat in the front passenger side of their car, staring at him, but big Bertha who sat in the back seemed nice. The Miller's even went to Eugene's door, introduced themselves and handed his ma a specially printed invitation with a real balloon inside. The Miller's had come back the next weekend to take Eugene to their house for the first party Eugene had ever been to.

Hell, Eugene's ma was thrilled to get rid of one of her kids for the afternoon. She tried to get them to take the other two. The Miller's had cake and ice cream and hot dogs grilled in the backyard. Shermy had a tree house with a rope ladder and a little dog named Toby who jumped through a hula-hoop whenever Sherm told him to—and the dog slept in Shermy's bed. Bertha had made the party boys play Pin-the-Tail-on-the-Donkey at that first party when most of them just wanted to run wild playing with all of Shermy's things—even that pansy ventriloquist doll. Eugene had thought he made that red nosed thing talk pretty good. Eugene's lips didn't move at all—Bertha had told him so. She sent him home with some of Sherm's clothes which he'd outgrown. Shermy was bigger than Eugene—most of the guys were. And sometimes, when he'd go to Shermy's to play, Bertha would make him take a bath and tell him to be sure and get behind his ears. One time she had trimmed his toenails. She combed his hair a lot and told him he was one handsome fella just like her Shermy!

Eugene smiles when he thinks of Bertha, but it made him sick to see those old people devoting their lives to that fat little kid with the stick-out ears. Some guys are such pussies. Usually there's a woman back there orchestrating the whole thing—turning a boy into a pansy. Sherman Sr. didn't really have much to say about it. It was Bertha who was flapping her lips and acting all sweet to everybody. Sherman, Sr. could have put a stop to it and toughened up the kid like Eugene's dad did for him and he's doing for his boys. Obviously big Bertha ran that show.

Eugene toots his horn at Charlie Yates who's out to his box getting his Sunday *Citizen-Times*. The *Old Country Music Hour* is on Eugene's station and they're playing *Wolverton Mountain*. Hell, that ain't so old, Eugene thinks. He remembers hearing that on the radio when he was a kid and it was rock 'n roll then. "People are always playing around with the facts," Eugene says out loud. I hate that, he thinks, as he slips a wad of tobacco under his lip. "I hate it when people play around with the goddamn facts."

121

Eight

"Reedville Woman Megabucks Winner" Charlie reads the headlines of the *Reedville Citizen-Times* as he heads back toward the house. He takes his time. He couldn't hurry if he had to. The best he can do is a slow shuffle. A sighting of Eugene Trueberry always upsets him—more like depresses him. Eugene has who Charlie wants and Eugene doesn't deserve Elizabeth, those boys, *his* son.

Charlie thinks he may not be able to stand living like this much longer. He's a brokenhearted man. He just put it into words last week—brokenhearted. He knew he'd been feeling worse and worse, but he didn't know how to put it—more desperate and hopeless. He couldn't find the right way to put it until it hit him. Brokenhearted! Charlie stops in his tracks, thinks maybe he can't make it to the house. She can't let go of that foul man and he can't understand why. And he can't understand why she can't tell Jimmy that Charlie is his father.

Not in a million years when he was young would Charlie have thought his life would go the way it has, bringing him to this point. When he saw Sarah at that auction, he was a young man full of hope. She followed him around that day, giggling, with her visiting cousin. It unnerved Charlie. He'd never been around a girl like that. His mother had tried to coax him into asking Dory Pierce to some of the dances. He couldn't muster the courage—couldn't dance, anyway.

Sarah wasn't shy. Sarah masterminded the courtship. She was feisty, determined against her parents wishes to marry Charlie Yates. He never knew what she saw in him. She could have had others—good looking, successful town boys like her parents wanted. Instead, she picked out a shy, country boy with no interest in living "correctly" as she put it.

Things are going to hell around here, Charlie thinks, as he looks at the garage which should have been painted two years ago. He looks at the downspout that is dangling from the eaves on the side of the house. He needs to get out the ladder, get up there and repair it. Basically what it boils down to is that he plain don't give a damn about much of anything any more.

Charlie picks up his heavy-booted foot and wills it to follow the other to the house. As he opens the door on the enclosed back porch, Charlie throws the paper on top of the freezer chest. There's a whole bunch of them piled up there. He doesn't read the paper anymore. He should cancel his subscription. The freezer's empty. Charlie unplugged it when he took out the last of Sarah's peaches. It has become a surface on which to pile papers.

The stray cat that's living on the enclosed porch walks over and rubs her mouth on his pant legs. She's a pretty little thing now that she's got all of those burrs pulled out of her long gray and white fur. He called her "Sorry" for several weeks. She looked so sorry when he first saw her. She was half starved, wormy, with a big gash in her leg and four kittens forming inside. She lost those kittens and almost her own life. Charlie had a huge bill at the vets. He couldn't believe he'd spent that kind of money on a stray cat when he'd had a barn full of them at times, and they took care of themselves—lived, died—and he hardly noticed.

This one's wormed her way into his life. She was real shy at first. Little by little, they got to know each other. Now, he calls her Blossom. He made a hole in the side of the porch for her to get out, but she pretty much stays right here. She's got it good and she's not about to lose it.

Charlie bends over to stroke her back as he sits down on an old metal lawn chair. Blossom jumps up in his lap and starts to purr in his ear. Sarah's rubber boots are still over in the corner. When her sisters came for the funeral they took some of her things—whatever they wanted. They left much behind. He should gather it up and take it to Goodwill or Sarah's church for their rummage sale.

Blossom nests on Charlie's cushiony lap. Charlie will probably get invited again to the Rankins for Christmas. He may turn them down this year with some kind of excuse. They're nice enough and the dinner is delicious but the whole thing—the kids and grandkids, the packages, the holiday spirit, the music—it leaves him feeling worse, hollow. It makes him too aware of what he's missed. Maybe he'll cook up a turkey for Blossom. He can probably do that. He'll ask Elizabeth how to do it the next time she sneaks in for a visit.

Elizabeth is a good cook. She brings him food all of the time. If it weren't for her he'd be eating cereal every morning, bologna sandwiches every noon and soup every night along with a lot of other junk. He eats a lot of snack things. He feels like he needs something to crunch on all of the time. Sometimes he eats over at the Crossroads Cafe. The food's good there. Their sausage gravy is the best around. Charlie never gets indigestion from it like he has at other places.

The worst time for Charlie is winter. There's not much to do on the farm. So many dark days. He and Elizabeth see less of each other. It gets complicated when there is snow on the ground. How would she explain tracks back on the lane? She walks down the road and cuts in across a field some of the time. Now that Sarah is gone, Charlie can pick her up down her road and drive her back to his house by going around the mile square. Tracks are always a problem. Often they meet at the cabin for old time's sake, and because they feel safer there for some reason.

It has been so hard all of these years wanting to make Elizabeth and Jimmy his family and not even coming close. He's even told Elizabeth that Will was welcome to come home from Indiana and join them. He said he'd treat him as his own just like Jimmy—if Will was receptive.

He wonders why, but he has to admit he loved Sarah, too. Even at the end he loved her. She was a bitter and vindictive woman who for many years made his life miserable. She wasn't loud or harsh. She was cold and withdrawn. It was like living all those years sealed in that deep freezer. But he felt responsible for her. In the early years when they both still had hope, Charlie adored her, could barely believe that she chose to be his wife. She was independent, so full of energy, and she could do anything on the farm. She helped plow in the spring, harvest in the fall and everything in between. Her parents hated seeing her work like that, dressed up in coveralls, smelling like a farm hand. They told her it was why she had trouble becoming a mother. She'd spent too much time in dirt and dung.

They were a team for several years—until the miscarriages and the birth. Charlie can't exactly remember when he sensed that he was losing her. It happened over several years. When she was thirty-five, a baby was born and died. Sarah moved to the room in the front of the house and locked her door every night. It was a loud click down at the end of that hall, every night, a *loud click.* Charlie never knew how badly a person could feel until that time in his life when he heard that click every night. She acted like he wasn't in pain, too, over losing their child. Like it was her sorrow, alone—as if she was the only one suffering. The doctor thought she was too old to try any more and recommended a hysterectomy because of all her problems.

Sarah came home from the operation a different woman. Charlie talked adoption. She shut the door. Click.

Charlie puts Blossom off his lap. He'll get her some nibblets, he thinks, or whatever they call that stuff. "I'll be back, Blossom," he says to her as she looks up at him with *big, green orbs*. Charlie grins as he looks into her eyes. He sees a *being* in there. He never realized that animals are beings until Blossom came. You can't recognize animals as *beings* and be a farmer. He's raised and killed many and sent hundreds off to the slaughter house. He wasn't a big time beef producer, but he always had a respectable herd. Their death supported his and Sarah's life. Now he thinks about when he took the calves away from their mother to wean them. The mother cows stood in the spot where they'd last been with their infant and bawled for two or three days. It bothered Sarah. She'd shut windows and turn up the radio. It didn't bother Charlie—other than to disturb his sleep.

He opens the door and looks back at Blossom. She makes a squeaky meow. She's trying to communicate something. Charlie thinks he's too dumb to understand. She sits her back end down. Blossom's big, fuzzy tail mops the floor behind her. Charlie thinks she looks like she's expecting him to do something. Should he say what he's been wanting to say for several weeks and can't believe that he's about to? "Would you like to come in, Blossom? Would you like to eat in the kitchen?" he queries. Blossom stands up. Walks right in. When he shuts the door behind her, she gets frightened and runs back, wanting out. Charlie opens it and she rushes out, skidding to a stop on the other side. He looks at her and says, "Wouldn't you like to come in, Miss Blossom?" Blossom is sashaying back and forth, seriously thinking about it. Charlie takes his coat off and hangs it on a hook. He leaves the door open a crack.

Blossom's nose appears in the crack and then, her face. "Come on in. It's warmer in here." He goes to the cupboard and tears open one of those little pouches. Blossom knows that sound and a little more of her body comes through the crack. Charlie puts the nuggets in a bowl and places it on the floor in the middle of the room. Blossom is still considering the situation. Charlie goes to the front room and sits in his recliner. This house is dead, he thinks. There's so little life here. There may as well be no life at all.

The best way he can describe how he feels is gray and flat. The whole world seems gray and flat. It has been that way for so long that sometimes it seems normal. The only joy in his life is when he's with Elizabeth. It's always so short lived. Their time together is sporadic and measured. They've never been together for more than four hours at a time. Sometimes between visits it's days but mostly it's weeks. Elizabeth has to feel that it is a safe night. Everything has to fall into place. I can't go on like this any longer, he thinks. When he thinks that, he knows what he means—sell the farm and leave. She won't leave. He will.

Charlie throws his head back. It has come to this, he thinks. I'm getting to be an old man and I'm all alone. I never saw it coming to this when I started out. All I ever wanted was a family on this farm. His mother and father and his brother who died at twenty are all over there in the township cemetery along with Sarah and little Patricia Marie, not far from Elizabeth's Terry.

"Hello there, Blossom." She jumps into his lap. Charlie strokes her as she purrs.

It was nineteen years ago when Elizabeth came into his life. She was just a girl. She'd been married less than a year. She'd just had a baby. It was back at his dad's old hunting shack. He'd taken to going there sometimes at night to get out of the house and away from the gloom that hung over it. Sarah didn't even know he was gone. By then she was locked in her room. He was forty-one and Elizabeth was around twenty.

127

It was April tenth. He looked at the calendar that night and never forgot. April tenth, their anniversary. He heard a tap on the door and when he opened it, there she was with her brown hair flowing to her waist, holding a sleeping baby boy. She had the creamiest complexion but that didn't register until later. All he got was an impressionistic vision of a beautiful young mother with a yearning in her voice.

"I was out for a walk, tryin' to put the baby to sleep. He's been real fussy and I saw the light," she said. Charlie stepped back from the door and Elizabeth walked into his life. She sat on the bed without a word, still cradling the infant Will. Charlie sat back in his rocker and they both sat in silence. Neither one of them are jabberers.

Suddenly Elizabeth stood up and brought Will who was fussing over to Charlie, placing him in Charlie's big, soft lap. Charlie was dumbfounded. Instinctively, he held Will in his arms and rocked. He wondered at that moment, did she know his life, his loss, his pain?

A few months later, she told him that she'd been watching him through the little window. It made him feel self-conscious, so she said that all he'd been doing was rocking in the rocker and watching the fire in the stove. She said, "You looked like a picher on an old Saturday Evening Post—a picher by that famous artist that does those real homey ones with freckle faced kids and real lookin' people and their pets. I knew I wanted to be a part of that picher—beside that stove with you."

How can something so innocent, tender and loving be so wrong? Charlie knows there are a host of people in the community who would jump to answer that question. They'd quote the bible. Charlie never dreamed he'd take a lover, let alone one twenty years younger—the wife of a neighbor—then, purposefully sire a child with her—Jimmy was no accident—and then to love her secretly for nearly twenty years. It's

128

crazy when he thinks about it like that. Absolutely crazy. Things like that happen in books not in real life, not *his* life.

The phone rings. He thinks about letting it ring out, even if it's her. But, Charlie gets up and carries Blossom with him. When he gets close to the phone, it rings. Blossom leaps to the floor. She's out the crack in the door in a split second. The kitchen is cold from leaving the door open. Charlie pushes it shut with one hand and answers the phone with the other.

"Hello?"

"I'm calling about the tractor you have advertised in the paper. What kind of condition is it in?"

Charlie had forgotten that ad would be in today. After he gave the guy all of the information, he was still interested; so, they set a time for him to come over and look at it. After hanging up Charlie realizes in the pit of his stomach that he'd taken the first step toward leaving. He took it last week when he placed the ad. He rubs his hand across his face and looks to the southwest. She's over there beyond that woods, between him and Arizona.

Maybe he should save the tractor for the auction. There will be a farm auction. The more he thinks about it the more he realizes that the ad is not his first step. He's been thinking about this for a while. He talked about it to Elizabeth. His *first* step was after Sarah died when Elizabeth said she couldn't leave Eugene; so Charlie sold his herd because he couldn't figure out why he should work so hard for nothing.

He asked Elizabeth to leave Eugene. He said he would set her up in her own house and they could pretend to have begun seeing each other after a respectable time. No one would have to know that she left Eugene for him. He said, "I need you. I want you to be my wife. I want to spend the rest of my life with you." She didn't say anything at first. Then, she said, "I'd better put this meat away. I'll get the container, later. I need that container. It's the only one I have left from the set I ordered from . . . "

Charlie can't remember what she said after that. He knew from the very beginning that he'd never have her. He knew it in his head but his heart beat in bliss, never getting the message to back off and let her go, free himself. Lord, he didn't want to be free of her! He simply couldn't accept why life had to be this way. Why can't she tell that pile-of-crap husband of hers to take a hike? If he ever hurts her again, Charlie might lose it. It was all he could do to restrain himself when she told him some of the things Eugene has done over the years. She says Eugene's leaving her alone now—has for several years since he started having trouble— Charlie almost thinks the words, "making love." Shoot, Eugene's never "made love" to her.

Eugene's not dependent on Elizabeth like Sarah was on Charlie. Why couldn't she leave or tell him to get out? He feels like he's been a big dumb fool, but he doesn't regret a moment of the time he had with her despite the fact that she poisoned him with her love—killed hope. It turned out that sweet and innocent Elizabeth Trueberry was, for Charlie, a very dangerous woman. If it hadn't been for her, he thinks, maybe he could go on now to find a nice widowed woman down there in Arizona. But no one will ever measure up to his Lady Elizabeth. He's been ruined, spoiled by passion, knowing how deeply one can love and desire another.

Charlie wants Jimmy to have this farm. If he inherited this farm and his father's sixty acres, boy, he'd really have something. That's the way it should be. How can he will the farm to some kid he doesn't hardly know? He's got to get that figured out somehow and into a will.

Charlie grabs his jacket and heads out to the barn to start the tractor. It should be warmed up before that interested party comes. It will start better and sound better. Blossom follows after him as he crosses the barnyard. The forsythia bushes around the house and the one out in the yard have gone wild. Someone should trim them next spring, he thinks.

Maybe he should go down to Arizona right now, before Christmas. Then he wouldn't have to make any excuses to Bob or Marjorie about Christmas. He knows Marjorie won't let it drop until she knows that he's got a place to go. If he goes to Arizona now, he could get something lined up down there and come back in the spring to get ready for an auction. He looks down at Blossom who shot out in front of him, leaping through the snow. "What will we do with you?" he asks his little companion.

He slides the barn door over enough to let himself through. "Have you explored this place, Blossom?" he asks her. "Lots of mice!"

Charlie hoists himself up onto the tractor. Maybe when he gets to Arizona he'll lose some of this weight. Charlie is breathing pretty hard by the time he gets up there. He turns the key on his Ford. It starts right up. It's been real reliable and should make somebody a nice all—around tractor he thinks.

Charlie looks up to the rafters. He remembers that day when he thought about ending it all . . . before Elizabeth came into his life. He was going to jump from the loft with a rope around his neck. Farmers do it that way all of the time. He hasn't really known any, but it's a pretty classic way to end it on a farm. People in town hook hoses to the car exhaust and asphyxiate themselves or they blow their brains out. Men, it's men who blow their brains out—males everywhere of all ages. It's probably because they're not cleaners and they don't want any chance of surviving. Women who do most of the cleaning like neater, less violent methods like pills which don't always work. Women want it both ways. To kill themselves slowly with the hope that it won't happen in the end. Men are comfortable with guns and ropes. Women, pills.

Charlie knows of a family whose teenage son blew his brains out and they wouldn't let anyone help them clean up the mess. He heard their next door neighbor say that she watched those parents all day long go in and out of the house—coming out on a regular basis with a bucket of pink water and pouring it into the grass behind the house. The neighbor men wanted to do it for them, but that mother and father, he heard, would have had a fist fight with anyone who tried to stop them.

Oh, lord! He'll never forget that day that he was back in his field when he heard the sirens going to Elizabeth's. He ran like a bat out of hell to that house. He got there a few minutes after the volunteer fire department's rescue truck. He didn't see Terry. He never saw the little boy. Sam and Harold from the squad were already hovered over him. Eugene was over by the barn, running in circles with no shirt on. Elizabeth lay crumpled in the grass, and Jimmy was standing near her hysterically crying. Charlie bent over to check on Elizabeth. She was breathing. Two more volunteers arrived and started working on her. Charlie kneeled down and for the first time in three years, held his son. Elizabeth used to sneak him back to the cabin with her whenever she could, but as soon as Will who had to come with her got old enough to start talking, it had to stop. When Terry was born, she was so overwhelmed with children that they couldn't see each other very often.

Charlie wouldn't know how to describe his situation that day when he ran to her farm. Elizabeth was overcome, passed-out in the grass. Her baby was dead. Charlie's wasn't. And he was cradling his son. He was there for his son when Jimmy needed his father the most.

Elizabeth was "out of it" for a couple of months. He didn't know what the heck was going on with her. He couldn't see her or console her. It was hell. She was lost in her house—in her bed, on medication. Sarah took a baked chicken over and some of her canned goods. A few days later she took a tuna and macaroni casserole and the next week, he thinks it was zucchini bread. Sarah never did see Elizabeth. Her sister Rose was there to receive things at the door.

There was an empty peanut butter jar on the counter at Buddy's as well as at Brown's Country Market like there always is when someone dies. The spiral notebook beside it said, "Contributions for the bereaved family of Terry Trueberry." When people put some money in they sign their name. The money and the sheet go to the family after a week of sitting on the counter. It seems to Charlie like there is always a jar on the counter in those places. Somebody that you know in some way or another is always dying. There was one for Sarah. It doesn't matter if you need the money. You can give it to charity. It's something somebody started years ago.

Charlie gets off the tractor. Blossom follows him across the yard, leaping through the snow and stopping every now and then to shake the cold wet off her paws. When Charlie gets to the field and keeps on going toward the cabin she stops. She watches him get smaller and smaller until she decides to go back to the porch. On the way she jumps on a leaf that skips across the top of the snow. A car goes by on the road. Blossom looks that direction. Her long fur blows toward one side of her body as she feels the coldness of the day hit her on her gray and white side. Her instincts tell her she is vulnerable.

Charlie shakes out the quilt from the bed in the cabin. He folds it and lays it in the rocker. He picks up the lantern and sets it out on the little porch. He scoops the ashes out of the heat stove and dumps them in the woods a little ways from the cabin. It will take some doing to get this iron stove back up to the house. He'll wait until it's closer to the auction and hire some young guys to help him get everything squared away. Maybe the auctioneers do that kind of stuff—move things around, out to the yard and into the barn.

There isn't much to take back to the house, a couple of quilts and the lantern. He'll get the rocker later. The bed isn't worth moving. All of a sudden, Charlie realizes that he's never looked into the cabin from the window on the side—the window through which Elizabeth first saw him. He walks around to the side and looks in but all he can see is his face. The light is not right. The window is a mirror and Charlie doesn't want to look at that old man. He doesn't want to believe that's him there in that glass—that fat-faced, old man. If he tries really hard, he can see himself as a boy. His eyeballs are the same but everything else has changed so much that he thinks he could be mistaken for someone else. He asks, plaintively, *"How . . . did this happen?"*

Charlie hasn't cried much in his life, but he can tell his eyes are moist. His eyelids are heavy. His chest is tight—very tight. He feels weak and tired. He goes back into the cabin and lays down on the bed. The springs moan as he puts himself down onto his back. He thinks of Arizona. He thinks that maybe if he tried really hard, he could be happy in the southwest but not in one of those big retirement villages. He doesn't want a bunch of dying old people around him in prefabricated boxes, lined up on curlicue streets. He wants kids and young families and middle-aged people as well. When he gets settled in, he'll eat better. Maybe he'll learn to swim or he'll join a club, be in a barbershop quartet—it has been years since he heard himself sing. *"Home, home on the range,"* eeks its way out. Maybe he'll sail a boat across . . . across the desert . . . wind blows in the desert, you know . . . God! . . . God! . . . Elizabeth . . . ohhhhhhh

Charlie's heavy-booted foot falls off the bed and hits the floor, hard. *And there is nothing to be done to stop the sun from setting on one's day . . . as it rises on another's.*

Nine

You cannot rely on anyone to do what they say they're going to do. That's what Bruce thinks as he knocks on the back door, again. A cat scurries behind the freezer. Bruce thinks she looks scared. He's seen that look on the stray cats that have come around his house. They can't get close. Cindy keeps cat food in bowls out on the deck. Off and on a stray cat comes to eat, but when you turn on the light or open a door they're gone.

Bruce decides to walk to the barn after he sees tracks in the snow going there. The barn door is open. He looks in and calls, "Anybody here?" There's the tractor. Bruce looks it over. Pretty good, he thinks. It's what he's been looking for, a newer model Ford. His is a '53. When they get that old— it's iffy. It's all he could afford at the time. Now he wants to move up. He's got to have one to drag logs, haul wood up to the house, plow snow off the drive and grade it after hard rains. This one has a gas engine. It's a '68, according to the ad. After '70 they're diesel. He doesn't want a diesel.

Bruce looks at the tires. Good. This guy's taken pretty good care of it. At least he kept it under shelter. Some of these farmers are sloppy with their machinery maintenance. Maintenance is everything in caring for any piece of machinery. People in general are sloppy about maintenance. Bruce would like to find the guy who lives here. He wants to listen to the engine and test the hydraulics, brakes and clutch. He prefers to buy from a dealer. That way if there

135

are any problems, he can take it back and demand some repair or compensation. A business has a financial future at stake. Private owners don't give a damn. Still, he'd like to talk to the guy, if he could find him. This is so close to home that he wouldn't have to pay to have it hauled. The guy would be right here if something went wrong, and he had to get hold of him.

Bruce leaves the barn. He sees the cat over at the house. She scurries through a hole back onto the porch. "Anybody home?" he yells toward the house. This really burns him up. People are so unreliable. Time wasted! Bruce heads for his car. From the looks of the place, Bruce begins to wonder about that tractor's engine. The more he looks around, the more he decides that this guy's *not* into maintenance. That's getting easy to see. That tractor may look good on the outside but be full of gunk on the inside.

Bruce gets into his new black truck. He loves that smell. A black truck is going to be hard to keep clean while driving on these gravel roads. Even if he goes real slow it gets dust and mud on it. Gravel and black don't go together, but it was so pretty and he got a good deal. He'll trade it off in two years, anyway. You don't want to lose your equity because of the mileage getting too high or the vehicle getting too old. This one handles better than the last, and he likes the quality of the radio.

He pushes the button. *" . . . don't love me any more, but please don't walk out that door. When we said I do, did you mean it, too?"* This is his regular station but the songs all sound different these days. They're playing more sad ones. So many sad love songs. It's unbalanced in that direction.

One more week and it will be Christmas vacation. Whoopee! If he can make it through the damn week, he'll have two weeks of vacation. After that—he hates to think about it. That stretch from January to spring vacation is murder. The kids are all bored. Everybody has cabin fever. He goes to school in the dark and shortly after he gets home, it's dark. When he does get to see the sky, it's gray. Last winter, there was a record in Michigan. Three straight weeks with no sun. Over twenty-five years he's been getting up at five-thirty and at six-forty driving to Reedville Senior High to watch the quality of kids go down along with his patience.

God, he'd love to live in Montana or Wyoming. Big Sky country! Cindy won't consider going west. She said if she goes anywhere it will be east. He never wanted to live in such a populated state as Michigan. He wanted to go even farther west than where he grew up in Kansas. Michigan's not as bad as New Jersey or Connecticut. He's never been there. But, he knows he wouldn't want to live there. He never intended to come east of the Mississippi. He doesn't want to think about that any more. Too depressing, he thinks, because it's too damn late.

"Don't you know, I love you so? Please don't go!" This has always been his favorite station. Why have they started playing depressing songs all the time? He could understand once in a while but all the time? Surely people have called in to complain about it. Cindy hates country music—says she always has. That's what she said the other day. He never knew it. For twenty years, he never knew it. She never said a thing until now. She hates country music! He realized she didn't like it the way he does, but he never thought she hated it.

If he and Cindy were getting along and she liked country music, he could get her to call the station and complain. She's the one who does stuff like that. Once she'd called a cat food manufacturer to ask if they'd changed the formula on their dry food because the cats didn't like it any more. Then she'd registered a complaint saying that her cats prefer the old formula over any other brand and would they please consider changing back. Does she actually believe, Bruce wonders, that some big company cares what she thinks? Several letters went back and forth. She did some research and found out that one canned pet food manufacturer was using the carcasses of pets killed at county and city pounds as meat. The rendering companies would pick them up and sell them as meat to a pet food cannery. Boy, that got her going! She crusaded on that tangent for several months. Phone calls here! Phone calls there! Letters! Meetings with her humane group! She got real crazy again and Bruce didn't see much of her for months. She had tried to turn her pets into vegetarians with some special recipe of oatmeal, carrots and other stuff. She can't cook a meal, but she was mixing, seasoning and cooking pet food for weeks. Neither the dogs nor the cats would eat it and she found out that the cats could die without some enzyme they get from meat. Another one of her crazy, do-gooder ideas gone amuck after a hefty investment of time and money and after abandoning Bruce for months.

Cindy hides out in that studio. She's always down there. She always acts busy. Like painting is important or hard work. He doesn't care what kind of money she gets for them. She doesn't do it enough to call it a job. She needs to get a job and contribute more. It's not fair that she gets to fool around like that all day and he has to go to work. Damn! He wishes he could fool around all day!

It's hard for him to remember anymore what it was like when she cut wood with him and helped stack it every Saturday morning. She used to walk the woods with him every Saturday afternoon after lunch. They'd have Campbell's split pea soup, a cheese sandwich and two chocolate chip cookies. Cindy would pick out the little cubes of ham from the soup. He'd eat them. They didn't bother his stomach. Then, they'd go for a walk. Cindy wanted to walk down the road sometimes, but that was crazy. Who would walk on the road when you have twenty acres of nature to roam?

They'd walk to the back of the property and Bruce would target practice with one of his pistols or rifles. He'd shoot a round and then walk up to the target to see how he did. He'd shoot another round and walk up to the target, again to see how he did, again. And, once again, like the cutting of wood, Cindy participated at first, even shooting. Then she'd get so she'd watch him shoot and with him, walk up to the target. Next thing you know, she had started bringing a magazine to look at while he shot and had sat there on a log while Bruce walked back and forth to look at the target. Eventually she stopped going with him. "Too much to do!" He figures she lost interest because she couldn't shoot very well. She lost interest in wood cutting because she wasn't strong enough to split the wood. All she could do is watch him and then load it in the wagon. She's never been content to play the supportive role. She wants to be the star.

They used to ride around every Sunday afternoon—for years, every Sunday afternoon, exploring the country roads. They did it every Sunday afternoon for years. They knew all of the roads in this county and the four surrounding ones like the back of their hand. He'd drink a diet coke and have a snack pack of cheese crackers every Sunday afternoon. She'd have a coke and a snack pack of pretzels every Sunday afternoon—every Sunday afternoon for years.

Every Friday night for eighteen years, they'd eat out. They'd eat at Papa Joe's in Vicksburg. Bruce didn't like to eat in Reedville. His students would either be working in the restaurant or eating there, and he doesn't feel like being around his students if he isn't getting paid for it. They'd get a medium pizza with mushrooms and green olives. She'd want black olives. Everybody knows they have no taste. She'd want onions, but nobody cuts them up into small enough pieces and they never get cooked enough. She'd want green peppers. His stomach can't handle green peppers. They don't taste good anyway. At Papa Joe's you pay for each ingredient—even if you only want it on half of the pizza.

Neither of them could tell you why, but for a three-year period they switched to Chuck's Subs and Brew. They'd each get a salad and a vegetarian sub. He'd order his without the onions, pickles, hot peppers or green peppers. Those all bother his stomach. She'd pick the hot peppers off when hers came. He couldn't understand why she didn't order it without the peppers. He'd watch her pick them off every week—always wondering why she didn't order it without the peppers. It became a moot point one night when they found themselves back at Papa Joe's ordering a medium mushroom and green olive pizza.

Bruce decides to drive to the auto supply store in Homer. He'll kill a little time and maybe stop back at that farmer's house later. Damn! The sun has come out. Bruce was hoping for a big blizzard. He hates Mondays. He starts getting depressed on Saturday evening when he remembers that Sunday brings Monday. In reality the only time of any week that he likes is Friday night. He feels like celebrating on Friday night. He drinks a little more that night. Four beers and two-and-a-quarter cups of wine. He measures it in a two-cup measuring cup and shoots it a little over the one cup mark. He used to stop directly on the one cup mark, but now he shoots a little over. It's closer to one-and-an-eighth cup. It's hard to tell because there is no mark for an eighth cup. He has a beer as soon as he gets home. He has the wine at four-thirty. They leave for the restaurant at five-thirty so they can be there at close to six. That's so they can avoid a line at the door and can be eating by six-fifteen or six-thirty for sure. He drinks two beers on the way to the restaurant. Cindy's his designated driver. That's the only time he lets her drive. They take her truck. He won't let her drive his. He drinks one beer at Papa Joe's. Then he comes home and goes to bed. He's in there by nine or nine-thirty, exhausted from the week.

Bruce looks at the farms as he goes by. He'd love to have been a farmer or a forest ranger. He'd love to be alone in nature all of the time. He'd worked on a farm for two summers in Kansas. He'd loved driving that machinery back and forth across those big fields. Day after day of back and forth. It was damn hot but peaceful. Nobody was hassling you. Everybody knows that you can only go so fast on a tractor across a field. All you have to do is keep the rows straight. It was hot and tiring, but he slept well at night. It's funny—even at night he went back and forth across those fields in his head. He still thinks about it when on a rare night he has trouble sleeping. He conjures it up. He goes back and forth. That was about the most peaceful time he's ever had. The next year after graduating, his old man had made arrangements for him to go to Ohio where his dad lived with his second wife and their two kids. If his dad was paying for college, he wanted Bruce where he could keep an eye on him. Bruce never wanted to become a teacher like his dad.

Meteorologist Pete Parker says on the acu-weather that there will be no snow tonight. A *chance* of flurries on Monday. Flurries! Damn! Probably just enough to make his drive into town a hassle. But there's still hope. It could happen later in the week. Bruce still has hope.

He decides he'd better drive to Buddy's and gas up. He only has a half tank in there. It's good for the vehicle to sometimes run it down close to empty, but Bruce has had trouble doing that lately. When he sees the tank get on half empty—or is it half full—he wonders—anyway, what does it matter, he *has* to put some gas in there. He's never been caught with his pants down—yet. He can't understand how someone could run out of gas. You keep your eyes on the gauge and you'll never run out. It's as simple as that! Some people are slobs about everything. They have no idea of how to conduct life. They don't know how to take care of business.

He sees that slipshod attitude in his students. And it can't be attributed to so many of them coming from single parent homes or being poor. He came from a single parent home when theirs was the only one in town. When everybody assumed that every kid had a dad at home. When "divorce" sounded like leprosy. His students have all kinds of good

141

stuff at their houses: VCR's, TV's all over the place, computers, video games, sports equipment, bicycles, radios, beds. How would they like to go to school in Kansas one whole winter in a spring jacket?

He has to constantly be on those kids backs about getting their name and class period in the upper left hand corner of the paper and the date in the upper right. And yes, neatness does count. It counts for a lot—that's something Cindy has never learned. It's apparent the way she keeps house. And knowing your dates is something that can really impress him at grade time. You have to know your dates in order to get it all in perspective. Otherwise you'd not realize the number of years separating the War Between the States and World War One. That's important if you want to understand your history. You've got to be able to look at it and really see where things fit on that continuum.

Cindy's floundering through life, floating on a paint brush. She doesn't understand the realities of life. She's always analyzing things. She's always trying to find ulterior motives or "interior meaning" as she puts it. And she's always getting it all wrong. He probably started this out all wrong when he invited her to marry him by saying that he always had leftovers after every meal. She got the idea from that that she could come up here, move in, eat his food and not contribute, like the pets. That's not what he was saying. He expected her to work. He expected her to teach. She had a teaching degree in art. It was too bad the art programs in the schools were all in cut back at that time. It gave her an excuse. When art teaching jobs finally opened up, she announced she didn't want to teach. She'd gotten that teaching degree only for her parents, like he had for his father. They realized she needed a practical skill like teaching—especially if you're going to major in art which was also a mistake on Cindy's part—art, how useful is that?

Now every once in a rare while, maybe five, six, seven times a year, she'll make a couple of thousand on a painting, usually less. He can't believe people would throw away that kind of money. But for some people it's easy come, easy go. She doesn't realize how long it takes him to earn the same kind of money with a whole lot more hassles. Those kids hate school just like he did. He hated sitting there day after day, year after year. It was so boring. When he was a high school student, he put in his time and went home—like now.

Cindy thinks she's got it bad. She *makes* her life bad. She chooses it. For example, the way she still cries about Marilyn disappearing. She can't let it be. She's always bringing it up—looking out the car window, hoping to spot her romping in someone's yard. Damn, it has been over a year. It's ridiculous to Bruce. When something is missing, he thinks, you consider it gone and forget it—quit looking for something that isn't there!

Sometimes Bruce thinks about getting on his Harley some day after school, driving west and disappearing himself. He wonders if she would look for *him,* cry for *him.* Chuck it all—all of the hassles. Cindy is always asking him questions, trying to probe his mind—looking for something that isn't there. That irritates him. He doesn't bother *her* like that. He's constantly having to fend her off. Your home should be the place where people leave you alone. That's Bruce's idea of domestic happiness.

"You can eat crackers in my bed anytime . . . " Now there's an okay song. He likes Barbara Mandrel—although he'd never allow anyone not even Barbara Mandrel to eat anything in his bed. Barbara Mandrel doesn't look like the type to do that.

Bruce pulls into Buddy's. Damn! The pump is in use on both sides. He pulls in behind an old Chrysler New Yorker—the one that was in his driveway on Thursday, the kid who was trying to dump some candy on Cindy. There's a gas guzzler, thinks Bruce. Maybe he should pull over to the other side and get behind the tan Honda. You can't tell which one will be done first. The Honda has a smaller tank, but maybe the

143

Chrysler is almost finished pumping. There are two teenage boys standing at the New Yorker, talking as the one holds the gas pump's nozzle. The kid may get it filled up and then stand there talking. Bruce had better pull around behind the Honda.

Bruce makes some old lady mad because he pulls out so abruptly. He's trying to get around to the other side before a car pulls in behind that Honda. He guesses he scared the old bat as she was walking to her car. She had plenty of room. He wasn't going to hit her. She simply wasn't paying attention until she saw his truck. She acted like he was trying to run her down. Bruce doesn't feel bad, though. She wasn't paying attention. He *was*. He gets in position behind the Honda and the girl pumping gas into it.

A blue Fiesta pulls up to wait behind the New Yorker. The guy who was talking to the kid walks away. The kid continues to pump. See, he knew it! The girl in front of him is finished! But so's the kid with the New Yorker who pulls the nozzle out and goes in to pay. The Honda girl takes a red, five-gallon gas can out of her trunk. She's going to fill that damn thing, too. Damn! First she waves to somebody and yells over at them with a big smile on her face. Damn! Get with it! She may not have anything to do but Bruce does. His time is precious.

The girl looks to be in her early twenties. It's hard to tell— damn hard. Some of those girls at Reedville High look like they're twenty-five or older. They don't act it, though— except when they're trying to come on to him. He doesn't do anything to encourage it. Any one of them could trump up some sexual abuse charge of improper touching or something and it would be up to him to prove them wrong. They say, "Hi, Mr. Mead," in a real suggestive, flirty way—especially when it's near the end of the grading period. He never acts even remotely friendly to any of his students—it could be misinterpreted.

The New Yorker pulls out and the car behind it pulls in beside the pump. The girl with the Honda puts her gas can back in the trunk. Bruce thinks about getting out to help her lift it, but she finally gets it in. Then she bends over through her driver's side door, probably getting her purse or getting money out of it. Whatever she's doing she's taking forever. If this were Bruce's dad sitting here he'd have laid on the horn—several times by now. *Finally,* she goes into the cashier to pay. A car pulls up behind him just as a truck pulls up behind the Fiesta on the other side of the pump. The Fiesta driver, a fat lady with three kids in the car, sends one of her kids in to pay and they're back in a flash. The car behind the Fiesta pulls up to the pump, presses the button and sticks the nozzle in. They probably only got two dollars worth. They pay and leave and the Honda girl still isn't back. Bruce wants to get over to the other side, but he's blocked in until the car behind him backs up a little and pulls in there . . . *on the other side.* That's it! He's out of here! Stupid-assed, sons-of-bitches!!!!! Bruce backs his truck up and gets out of there. He looks back—still no sign of the bitch with the Honda.

This is the way it always is. Bruce is always getting screwed. It's a cold world and shit is always happening. That's what Cindy doesn't realize. He's out here dealing with the world all of the time. Shit like this is always happening. She should stand in line at the grocery store—that'll kill anyone. Bruce could ring some necks in there. Those women are real bitches at the Save-a-Long. He means both the customers and the clerks. Even the stock boys are rude. He asked one once where something was and he got a real smart-alecky answer back. But he expected that from his experience with teenagers.

His stomach is starting to bother him. Damn! If Cindy doesn't want to ride around in the truck with him on Sunday afternoon, he'll do it by himself. He needs to get some gas, a pop, and some cheese crackers but not until about two-thirty or three. The snacks he means—he shouldn't have them until two-thirty or three. But he needs the gas now! His tank is half empty. He can't drive around half empty.

Ten

Jimmy's supposed to meet Starr around the bend from her house at two o'clock. He picks her up there a lot. She will jump out of the weeds and into his car. He knows the routine. She tells her parents she's real tired and she's going to bed. Then she puts her stuffed animals under her covers and goes out the window. Her parents trust her completely, she has told Jimmy. They say it all the time. "We trust you to do the right thing," they say, according to Starr, who had told Jimmy this once while they were riding around at about one in the morning. Starr had deadpanned, *I do the right thing.* They both snickered and snorted as they cruised their way to Reedville in Jimmy's New Yorker.

Now she's sneaking out in broad daylight. He doesn't know how she gets away with it. Jimmy doesn't care how. He's glad to be with her. They mostly drive around. That's why he got gas. Jimmy's pounding his thigh in rhythm to the music. He loves heavy metal. He'd like to let his hair grow real long, but his dad would never allow it. Man, it don't matter, Jimmy thinks. Over the music, he yells triumphantly, "'Cause I'm history 'round there after this year, man."

Starr told him on the phone last night that she's suspicious her parents are going to make her change schools next year. "I'll fight them," she said, "but, I have this feeling." Jimmy reaches into the back seat and gets the bag of chips he bought at Buddy's. He's drinking a Mountain Dew. Dew and Brew—his drugs of choice. Dew up. Brew down. Yeah!

Jimmy wonders what he'll get for Christmas this year? He wonders what that fucking Charlie Yates will give him? It'll be from his ma, *supposedly*. He got a great stereo and headset for his birthday. That pissed his old man off. Charlie paid for it, probably. Jimmy doesn't know for sure. He decided not to trash it like he did the Yamaha last year— since he didn't know for sure.

Jimmy pounds the steering wheel for this one. He loves this one. This station plays the greatest music and that Take-a-Hike Mike who deejays from two-thirty to four-thirty during the week. He's great. God, he's wild. Jimmy had a picture of him in his head. He had long hair, dyed black and a pierced nose. Then he saw a picture of him from the *Citizen-Times*. Jake Harman brought it to school to show around. "Take-a-Hike's" got short hair and he's fat and wears plaid shirts. But it doesn't matter to anyone because he has a cool head and a flaming mouth.

Jimmy's killing time until two. He can't go home. If he goes home he might get stuck there doing more chores. He'll go back to see Terry. He's already been there once today. But, that ain't no big deal. Some days—on the worst day—he was there for ten hours altogether. He left twice in that time. But altogether it was about ten hours.

Having this car for a year has been great! It gets him out of that house and away from those people. "Thank-you, Travis for fuckin' up! Thank-you Aunt Rose for givin' me your fuck up's car," Jimmy shouts over the music. He'd have never gotten a car if Travis wasn't doing time. Seems like with all the stuff Travis and Will stole, he could have gotten himself something better to drive.

Travis was a big druggie and drinker. Travis fucked up when he lost his cap at that head-doctor's house while he

148

and Will were grabbing that gun collection. Travis could have had a better car if he hadn't been into drugs. Will has a really hot Trans-Am. Will didn't get into the drugs. He liked alcohol. It's pretty cheap—especially if you steal it. Nobody could ever prove Will was at that doctor's house, although a lot of people including the cops suspected it. The guns were on Travis's property and it was his cap. Travis never squealed on Will. Jimmy and Will knew he wouldn't—they're blood. But the whole thing made Will jumpy. Jimmy thought Will might "crack up" over it—waiting to see if the cops were going to get him.

The township cemetery is a cool place to hang out unless it's memorial day or there's a funeral going on. Those days it's grand central station as Big Ma would say. Most days, it's peaceful. Jimmy can play his radio as loud as he wants. He plays it for Daniel James Riley, Born, August 16, 1903, Died, September 22, 1978 and Daniel's beloved wife, Mary Murphy Riley and for the Harpers who are Terry's neighbors on the other side. But, he really plays it for Terry Lee Trueberry, Beloved Child of God, Born, June 19, 1978, Departed, November 2, 1980. Jimmy wants Terry to know what good music sounds like since he didn't get a chance to grow up and find out.

Jimmy's ma believes Terry went to heaven. Jimmy thinks there is no such place. Starr doesn't either. Jimmy decided a long time ago that if there is a god he's mean and he's not about to get on his knees for somebody so mean. When he was little he went to church with his ma, every Sunday morning and Wednesday night, at Christ's Pentecostal Church over on Bailey Road. She's regular there. But she's finally stopped trying to make Jimmy go. It was okay when he was little. It's something to do when you're little and don't have anything else to do. Jimmy has plenty to do these days.

Jimmy drives past the big, shiny gray ball that marks somebody's grave. That was bold, he thinks, to stick that

149

thing in there among all these rectangles. People probably wanted to pitch a bitch about that rock ball. He knows people around here well enough to know that a ball-shaped headstone is to some people like flipping the bird.

He drives past the Hoyte's plot. They go way back to civil war vets. He toots his horn at Jeremy Hoyte. Jeremy was in the third and the fifth grade with Jimmy. When they were in the seventh grade, Jeremy was killed instantly in a car wreck. He always honks for Jeremy when he drives by.

Jimmy turns his radio louder as he gets closer to Terry. The vibration of the music is awesome. His whole car vibrates. Good thing there aren't any houses around here. They'd be bitching. The only thing he wishes is that Terry could have a big tree. He's out here in the newer area in the back and there aren't any big trees back here. It's hot in the summer sun. He also wishes Terry was next to another little kid. Yeah, he wishes that, too. These guys around him are all pretty old. Not that he would want any other little kid to croak. If Jimmy was god, only old people would die—forty and over.

Jimmy opens a pack of cigarettes. He decided the other day that he was going to start smoking. Sometimes he feels like such a retard. A lot of the other guys have been smoking for years. He doesn't smoke in front of Starr yet. He knows she won't like it. Fuck, she's probably leaving! What the fuck does he care what she thinks? She's got a bunch of plans for herself. She knows *right now* that she wants to do hair at *The Curl Up and Dye* in Reedville.

I don't know nothin' 'bout what I can do 'cept work on a farm, Jimmy thinks as he flicks his ashes out the window. He loves to flick ashes and he loves to hold the cigarette between his lips, squint his eyes and talk with it bobbing around. He watches himself do that in his rear view mirror. As he says, "Hey, Babe. What's up?" Jimmy thinks he's not too bad looking. He gets brown in the summer and has some good muscles from helping on the farm and working on two others. Sometimes he thinks that Charlie Yates should ask to hire him. Charlie could use the help. When Charlie asks Jimmy to work for him, Jimmy will say straight to his red face, "*Fuck you!*"

Jimmy wonders how Cindy Mead is coming with his story. He can't wait to read it. He wants it all down in black and white so he can hold it in his hands, hopefully get a grip on it. He thinks he should tell Cindy Mead to make his ma and Charlie real ugly. That makes him snicker as the cigarette bobs.

A car drives into the cemetery. Jimmy turns his radio up as he rolls up the window. The green car creeps along in the middle of the cemetery, and then turns at the first lane to the right. Jimmy's been expecting it. It stops in the old part. An old man gets out. It takes him forever to get out and shut the door. Jimmy's seen this guy a lot. He's out here every Sunday at about this time. Jimmy thinks of him as Mr. Sunday.

Mr. Sunday is bent forward at the waist and wears an old brown hat. It can be a hundred degrees and he'll have that hat on. And he wears long sleeve shirts in summer and suspenders. He's really old. He's too old to be driving. He weaves around in his lane and drives about fifteen miles an hour. It's all Mr. Sunday can do to keep his car on the road. One time Jimmy got behind him out on Fletcher Road and couldn't pass for a couple of minutes. It pissed him off. They ought to get those old fuckers off the road.

Jimmy takes another puff. He doesn't cough. His lungs are getting better, he figures. He coughed a lot at first. Maybe he'll offer Starr a cigarette. He knows she's against smoking, but so was he at one time. Just like he's against drugs now, but he may not be next year or next month. You never know what you're going to do. Jimmy's learned that much about life. You never know what's going to happen or what you'll

151

do. Starr might say "okay" when he offers her one. Jimmy gets excited when he fantasizes lighting her cigarette, flicking his Bic for her.

He'd give anything if he could kiss her—kiss her on that sexy, little mouth. It would probably ruin what he does get from her. She'd probably bolt. Maybe he could bring it up, somehow, that he wants to be more than her best friend.

Jimmy sits up in his seat and waves his hand back and forth in front of his face to clear the smoke. He thinks he saw something. He opens his window and as the air clears, he sees Mr. Sunday laying on the ground. Actually, he can only see a little of the arm of his brown overcoat waving in the air. The snow is banked there covering his view. Jimmy jumps out and starts to walk quickly down the lane. He thought maybe he saw it wrong, but then he starts to run across the snow toward Mr. Sunday who's down on his side.

The old man shouts, "Hello!" as Jimmy runs up to him. "I've gotten myself in a pickle here. I've fallen and I can't get up." This guy's a real comedian, Jimmy thinks, but he doesn't laugh. Jimmy asks, "You a *stand-up* comic?" Now, Jimmy laughs. Nobody could say Jimmy doesn't have a good sense of humor. Jimmy can be a comedian when he's in the mood which is hardly ever. Jimmy loves that TV commercial. The kids all make fun of it. That old lady is laying on the floor and then she says all pitiful, "I've fallen and I can't get up!" It's the way she says it. The commercial is for some medical thing that signals people if you need help.

"Where's your medical thing that signals people if you need help?" Jimmy says sarcastically. "You oughta get yourself one of those." The old man looks at him with his face all scrunched—like he's hurt. Now Jimmy's scared. What if he picks the old guy up and hurts him even more? He's seen on *Rescue 911* that sometimes you shouldn't move an injured person. "Where does it hurt?" Jimmy asks.

152

"Where it always hurts," the old man barks back. He's pissed off. "Where it hurts every day—in my knees and hands, in my back and left shoulder. Will ya help me get up or ya gonna let me lay here and freeze ta death?"

Fuck, this guy's no comedian. He's a fuckin' grouch, Jimmy thinks as he gets behind him and grabs him under the arms. He pulls the old guy up as far as he can. Mr. Sunday is no help at all. Most people would help themselves. They'd pull their legs under their body and push up. This guy's about as helpful as a sack of pig pellets and for being so shriveled up, he's heavy. Jimmy's struggling to keep him up. It's taking his breath away. This is harder than throwing bales of hay all day, Jimmy thinks still trying to hoist the old man to his feet. All of a sudden, while he's got him up there, expecting Mr. Sunday to get his legs in gear, Mr. Sunday slips out of his overcoat, falls back into the snow and leaves Jimmy standing there holding an old brown wool coat. Fuck! Jimmy thinks as he looks down at him sitting in the snow. Mr. Sunday's hat tumbles toward a tombstone which stops it from going any farther.

Mr. Sunday looks up at Jimmy and says, "Ya got a spare tire?" He's nutso, Jimmy thinks. Lost his marbles somewhere. To humor him, he answers, "Yea, right here!" Jimmy grabs at his sides above his waist, jumps up and down, giggling. His Aunt Rose is always grabbing at his Uncle Kink's side and teasing him about his spare tire. Jimmy's laugh makes him cough. Mr. Sunday does not laugh. He's thinking, crazy kid, kook, maybe even a doper. Mr. Sunday asks, slowly, "Ya got a spare tire . . . in . . . yer . . . trunk . . . not *on* yer trunk?"

A sober looking Jimmy, decides that *is* funny, but he's not about to give Mr. Sunday any satisfaction. Jimmy asks in a cocky tone, "Yeah, why?"

Like he's in charge, Mr. Sunday orders, "Go get it." Jimmy thinks this is pretty crazy and so he says, flippantly,

153

"Okay." He wants to see what the senile old fart will do when he shows up with the tire.

"Come back here with that coat!" Mr. Sunday barks. "Help me put it on!" Jimmy slips the coat back on the guy the best he can and starts back to his car, strutting at the same speed as when a teacher asks him to get back to his seat. He's like a car with a racing engine, gears engaged, but a foot slightly depressing the brake.

The old guy yells, "Pronto! I'm gettin' pretty cold. I got poor circulation as it is. I don't want it down ta *zero.*" Jimmy holds to a strut for a few more seconds on principle.

Jimmy pulls his car behind Mr. Sunday's. His car looks older than Jimmy's Yorker, but Mr. Sunday's car doesn't have any rust spots. He gets the tire out of the trunk. Jimmy throws it in the snow in front of Mr. Sunday. Jimmy puts his hands on his hips as if to say—so there! Jimmy feels like a parent must feel. He's lording himself over Mr. Sunday, who is helpless down there. Mr. Sunday looks up at him like a little kid who knows he's helpless. The look makes Jimmy angry. His dad would say, "Wipe that pussy, baby look off your face or I'm gonna smack it off."

"Put the tire behind me flat on the ground," Mr. Sunday orders, snapping Jimmy out of the bad mood that was about to devour him. "Now, get behind me, brace the tire with yer feet so it won't slide and pull me up onto the edge of it." Jimmy does it. It was easy. The old man is steadying himself with his hands on the tire, upon which he is now sitting. His legs are flopped out in front of him. "Now, get the keys outa my ignition and get my tire outa my trunk. I'll sit onta the edge here of your tire and you put my tire on top a this one. Butt it right up ta my back."

Jimmy does it but he can't see what's to happen after that. "Now you stand behind me there. Brace the tire with yer legs again. Reach across and drag me up onta this top tire."

Jimmy grabs Mr. Sunday under his arms from behind. "Just drag me back and up ta the top tire." Jimmy does it and it works, but for what? Mr. Sunday is now sitting on top of two tires, stacked in the snow in the cemetery.

"Now let go and see if the tires are stable like that." Jimmy lets go, but he's ready to grab if Mr. Sunday starts to fall. Mr. Sunday's brown spotted hands are cupped across the top of the tire. The tires are stable. He's stable. "Come up front here! Let me grab ya 'round the neck and you grab around me, under my arms." Oh, fuck! Jimmy thinks. They're going to be face to face and the old man probably has breath like Big Ma. He has a chin full of stray hairs like Big Ma.

"All I need is a good hoist *up*." With that, Jimmy bends his knees. His legs straddle Mr. Sunday's. He leans over and grabs the old guy around his waist locking his hands in the back. Mr. Sunday puts his arms around Jimmy's neck.

"Ready?" Jimmy asks.

"Ready," Mr. Sunday says and up they go. Mr. Sunday hangs onto Jimmy's neck way longer than Jimmy likes. He can feel the old fart getting himself stabilized. Still, if the old guy doesn't let go of him soon, he may throw up. "There!" Mr. Sunday declares. "We did it!" Mr. Sunday would slap Jimmy on the back if he could, as it is his hands are . . . gently patting . . . Jimmy's back.

"Just hang on ta me, son and help me over ta the car." They do a slow . . . slow . . . face to face free-form dance, courting disaster over to the car. A slow-motion jitterbug. Mr. Sunday is characterizing it in his mind as a jitterbug. Jimmy gets Mr. Sunday into the driver's seat. Panting with relief, Jimmy goes to the back of the car to put the tires away. "I'll just sit here fer a bit," the old man yells out.

"You better turn the heater on and wait to warm up before you drive," Jimmy warns as he reaches in and puts the key in the ignition. He figures the old man might have a hard time doing that since his crooked fingers are probably numb. Jimmy had brushed as much snow as he could off Mr. Sunday but the snow stuck to his coat and his pants were wet. It was more than melted snow on the brown pants. Where the old man had been sitting, Jimmy saw yellow snow.

Mr. Sunday turns the key and the car starts up. "Can I give ya somethin' fer your trouble?" Jimmy waves his hand back and forth in the air and says, "Nah," as he backs away.

"Thank-ya, son. What's yer name?"

Jimmy pauses for a second and says, "Dack. Dack Dick!"

"Thank-ya, Dack Dick. I sincerely, thank-ya." Fuck, Jimmy thinks, that's the first time in real life that anyone ever called me Dack Dick . . . and Mr. Sunday didn't look at him funny like Cindy Mead.

Jimmy sees Mr. Sunday's hat over by a headstone with a carved angel on top. "I'd better stay with you for a while," Jimmy says handing him the hat he retrieved. He goes around to the passenger side and opens the door. "Is that Okay?"

"Jump in," the old man says. Soon, the heater starts to warm things up and Mr. Sunday, whose real name is Lloyd with two "L's," Klumpp with two "P's"—two "L's" at the front, two "P's" at the end—is nonstop talking—slowly but with no breaks. That's his wife over there. That's who he comes to see every Sunday. She's been gone for eight years. Lloyd's kids all moved away years and years ago. A son lives in California. Another lives in Minnesota. A daughter lives in Florida. That one in Florida wants him to get out of the cold and live down there, but he won't go. He says, "I got ma freedom here. If I move down there, they'll be tellin' me

156

what I can and cannot do. They'll be tryin' ta take the car away. I know it. This here car's ma freedom, if ya know what I mean." Lloyd winks in Jimmy's direction.

Jimmy knows exactly what he means. Lloyd knows that he and Jimmy understand each other on that point. Lloyd turns to Jimmy as far as his torso will twist and says, "Ya got a girlfriend, Dack Dick?"

"Sorta."

"Sorta what?"

Jimmy picks at the seam of his jeans jacket and says, "Well, I got a real good friend who's a girl, but I don't think she'd like to be called my girlfriend."

"Well, Dack, life is hard. Seems like love should be the easy part. Believe me it's not. Lucretia and I went 'round and 'round a lot." Lloyd's finger twirls in circles in the air. "We had long periods of what ya'd have ta call livin' within a truce." Lloyd side-glances at his wife's grave. "Three of my grandkids," Lloyd blurts out, "divorced! Hardly been married and now they're all three divorced. People don't stick tagether like they used ta. Used ta, a woman wanted a roof over her head, a man wanted a fluffed-up nest and they both wanted a family. They stayed put."

"Yes, sir," Lloyd continued, "the heart is a touchy thing. I don't mean that muscle in the chest, although it can get touchy too. Mine's been touchy lately. But the symbol for love. Yes, sir, that love's a touchy damn thing."

"It's easiest ta love dead people, Dack," old Lloyd cracks as he points a long crooked finger over toward his wife's grave. "Ya can turn 'em into any kinda saint you want. It's like they go back ta bein' as innocent as when they came inta this world. They can't talk back, Dack. That might seem good ta ya, sometimes. But that's bad, really—ta be talkin' ta

157

someone who can't talk back. It's best ta tell your troubles ta the livin', if ya got someone livin'."

Jimmy can't look at Lloyd. Lloyd's talk is making him uncomfortable.

"It's funny how we all go back ta the beginnin' at the end— only we're not *cute*. We're pretty damned disgustin'. Wrinkled old people don't get pawed-over, Dack." He twists his torso, again which turns his head toward Jimmy. "In fact, people don't like ta touch us a'tall." Jimmy squirms. "They talk ta us like we was babies, and sometimes we have 'bout as much say in our lives as babies. Seems like nobody hears us." Jimmy can relate to that.

"People all start out life as bed ridden bein's, Dack. Then we start ta get mobile needin' assistance with standin' and walkin'. We fall a lot at first. Babies need walkers and other people ta support 'em for a while there. Life goes forward and then, goll dernit, if it don't go backwards to a walker, a chair with wheels and finally, a bed with rails and a rubber sheet."

Jimmy is studying the plowed drive in the cemetery. A squirrel runs down it, and leaps across some snow onto a tree.

"Ya begin to realize it in your gut right there in the middle— that yer slippin' away. Yer goin' back ta where ya come from—ya know it in yer gut that yer not immortal. Ya come ta discover *right there in the middle*, that you'll be the so-called *lucky* one, if ya get old enough ta be crippled and stinky, 'cause people *yer age* start droppin' dead all around ya. Then, in old age if ya got that far, there comes a point when ya know there's not much good comin' down the pike in your direction and there's no doubt about it. That's a blessin', Dack. It makes leavin' a tiny bit easier. Ya wake-up one day ta find ya don't know nobody yer age no more." Lloyd lifts the brown hat off his head and strokes what's left

158

of his gray hair. "Ya know a lotta people around yer age, don't ya, Dack—a whole school full?" Lloyd queries. Jimmy's head nods, slightly—just enough to let Lloyd know that he's been listening but begrudgingly.

"Whether we know it or not, every livin' thing—human and nonhuman cherishes life even those humans who think they got somethin' waitin' for 'em on the other side." Jimmy wants to smoke . . . or suck his fingers.

"When ya get old, Dack, ya need assistance standin' and walkin' just like at the beginnin' . . . Oh, lord," Lloyd throws his age-mangled hands up in the air and rolls his eyes back in his head, " and then, if ya fall, they wanta put ya back ta bed fer good." Lloyd looks sharply at Jimmy. "Ya won't tell nobody that I fell, will ya?"

"No way!" Jimmy firmly assures him, looking straight at him for the first time.

A relieved Lloyd Klumpp lowers his head. "At the end there, Dack, we whiz in our pants, again." Jimmy thinks he might laugh. He thinks he might cry. He's stuck right there in the middle teetering between the two until Lloyd belts out a big laugh. Jimmy laughs with him.

"But I had it good. Some people never make it ta old, Dack."

"I know! I know that!" Jimmy snaps at Lloyd. He looks down at the floor mat. Lloyd can tell that he does know.

"Who ya visit back there?" Lloyd asks. Jimmy sighs. The left corner of his mouth pulls back a couple of times before it straightens itself out and opens up to say, "My little brother, Terry. He died when he was two. I was four. I was with him." Jimmy says nothing for a few minutes. Lloyd doesn't grab the ball. He lets Jimmy take a time-out. His heart hurts for the big frosty kid who is beginning to melt on the seat next to him.

Jimmy looks out over the snow covered field beside the cemetery. He's afraid he's going to cry. He's trying hard to stuff it. Here he is sitting in old Lloyd Klumpp's old car and old Lloyd Klumpp calls him Dack Dick, and he's about to tell him his true story.

"We was playin' under my . . . " He stumbles on the next word, " . . . dad's . . . truck."

He corrects his choice of words and says, "We was playin' under a truck of the guy who until last year I thought was my dad and everybody still thinks . . . is—only now, I know the truth. We was playin' under that guys truck, but he didn't know it and he backed up missin' me, but . . . " Jimmy stops dribbling. Another time-out. He is hunched over his hands as his fingers rub furiously together.

"I seen it Lloyd. I seen it. I can still see it. The tire crushed his chest just as my red cowboy hat fell off his head. My dad raced into the house and come back out to Terry and then went runnin' 'round the yard hollerin' and yellin' that I shoulda knowed better. Ma, my ma come runnin' outa the house and fell in the grass. Then men started comin' just as I turned invisible."

"They was doin' things to Terry. Some was kneeling over ma. No one saw me. A couple was chasin' 'round after my dad or who I thought was my dad, tryin' to calm him down. And I just stood there frozen in my moon boots, like I was watchin' it from the moon—watchin' it until a big man grabbed me up and held me tight and said, 'Yer all right, son. Yer daddy will keep you safe.' And I felt safe as everything faded from sight 'cept that man's rough, thick, red neck which I stared at for hours—exploring it for hours like it was a piece of land with hills and low spots and dryed up creek beds which I traced with my finger."

Jimmy lifts his head and stares straight forward. "I seen it, Lloyd. I seen the tire crush his chest. I didn't know what it meant. I was between the tires, but . . . " Jimmy stops talking and utters one whimper. "It shoulda been me. I'm the **bastard** who shoulda died that day."

Lloyd grabs the ball and dribbles double time. "It shoulda been neither one a ya, Dack. It shoulda never happen ta anyone that young. He shouldn't have died. You shouldn't have had ta see it or be blamed fer it. And, yer dad . . . " Lloyd regroups to follow the boy's direction. "The dad shouldn't have had to experience such a tragic accident that would cause him to feel so guilty, so responsible for the *accident* that he tried ta blame *his . . . * " Lloyd changes his wording. " . . . *an* innocent child.

"Lloyd," Jimmy says softly, "what do you think of a man who's married to somebody for a long time and for over eighteen years of that time—what do you think of a man who over eighteen years on and off gets together with this married woman who has kids? What do you think of those people—that man and that woman who are married to other people? And"—Jimmy's not sure he can say this part—"What do you think of them if . . . if them two people who got together over that time—what if them people had . . . had them . . . a *kid together* and everybody thinks that the kid belongs to the woman's husband? What would you think of them two people?" Jimmy wipes a tear off his cheek by pretending to scratch his face. When he sees Lloyd studying him, Jimmy feels angry for being so overexposed.

Lloyd Klumpp is moving his legs around to get the circulation going. "Oooh, that's a tough one. That's a tough one." Lloyd rubs his chin with his fingers. Jimmy can hear the whiskers bristle. There's a long period when neither one of them says anything, but it doesn't seem to matter. Lloyd's lost in thought and Jimmy is patiently waiting. He doesn't even mind the smell of the old man's piss.

161

"In my youth, I wouldn'ta thought 'bout it one way or t'other. Somethin' like that never affected me—and if somethin' didn't affect me—it wasn't worth thinkin' about. Somewhere 'round thirty, I woulda thought it was a terrible thing ta do. It was kinda a way a keepin' myself in line by tryin' ta keep other people in line. 'Cause I had times when I wanted ta get out of line, Dack. Truthfully. I was envious a those who had the courage or stupidity—whatever it was ta get outa line. Somewhere in the middle years, I learned that I can't judge nobody. Doesn't mean I stopped judgin'. By then it's a habit. Ya know I do it every day—like I just did 'bout my grandkids gettin' divorced. But I know up here"—Lloyd taps his head with his first finger—"that there are too many factors that I probably don't know about. I finally figured out that I don't know much a nothin' and by knowin' that, I pretty much know the whole lot. Believe me, Dack Dick, tryin' ta understand life is not just difficult: *it's a wham damn doozy!*"

"I've read a lot in my life. That's why I thoughta those tires. I read an article last month about *leverage*. Anyway, there's one thing I've decided—nothin' is for sure. *The facts* and *the truth* are always up for grabs." Jimmy is wondering when old Lloyd is going to get to the point. Jimmy needs to pee and that's the simple truth. That mountain dew has run its course about like this conversation.

"I don't care what nobody says. Every cast-in-concrete *truth* is up for examination and often it doesn't hold up . . . it may hold up *now* but in three generations or next week be viewed as *superstition.*" Jimmy thinks Lloyd is starting to act a lot like the preacher at his ma's church. He's even waving his hands around to emphasize things.

"And there are so many forces pushin' an' pullin' against us. There is *no* one way and *no* pat answer." Lloyd slaps his boney thigh on both no's. But it barely makes a sound, just a dull *thud*. "Why just last week, I read in the paper that one *normal* isn't what it used ta be. A *normal* body temperature has been 98.6 degrees for years and years. Now, normal is considered ta be less than 97 degrees ta more than 99 degrees, and ya don't have a *fever* until it's up ta 100. *Normal* is definitely up for questionin' and interpretation."

"And, get this, Dack!" Lloyd gets animated at this. "The Vatican has just announced that its put some new *sins* on its list. They'll get those boozin', breeders shaped up yet. *And,* they," Lloyd says speaking softer like he's about to share confidential information, "they've decided, now, that Galileo wasn't a heretic after all." Lloyd laughs, raucously for an old fart who's been sitting in snow. "See," Lloyd points his finger at Jimmy, "See, we're all judgin' each other. It's parta the human condition."

Jimmy understands why Lloyd is talking about sinning, but he doesn't understand why Lloyd Klumpp is talking about fevers. "Yes, sir," Lloyd lets it out on a big sigh and then, he sings with a shaky but nice voice:

> *Here I go again,*
> *I hear the trumpets blow again,*
> *All aglow again,*
> *Takin' a chance on love.*

"Ethel Waters sang that in a play on Broadway called, *Cabin in the Sky* back in the early forties." He leaves it at that until he says, "Love between men and women, love between parents and children, love between anyone. Yes, sir, the heart's a touchy thing, Dack Dick. Love is a risky endeavor. Ya either follow yer heart or ya don't."

Then Lloyd says directly to Jimmy, "Look, son, whatever happened wasn't done ta hurt ya. That doesn't make it right or make it wrong. It's two hearts bein' touchy. Like you can't help lovin' that girl a yers."

Jimmy's face turns red. Suddenly, he feels like he's being buried alive inside Lloyd Klumpp's old car. The smell of

163

urine begins to nauseate him. It feels like it's a hundred degrees as beads of sweat form on his forehead. Jimmy needs to bolt and without debate, he does. Jimmy Trueberry, a.k.a. Dack Dick, opens the door and without saying good-bye to Llloyd Klumpp, a.k.a. Mr. Sunday, jumps into his car and guns it. It's amazing he hasn't run into a headstone, the way his car fishtails down the narrow lane.

Fuckin' old fart, Jimmy fumes. But he knows that he doesn't mean it. He likes the old guy. He hates that when he likes some old guy—some old guy like Charlie Yates. Oh god, Jimmy hits his steering wheel! How could he think such a thing? How could he think he could *like* Charlie Yates? He hates his guts. Jimmy's head feels real messed up. He knows he's going to do another drive-by viewing. When he does he goes real slow. Could he actually someday get to know Charlie? Talk to him like he talked to Lloyd Klumpp? Could he actually someday be okay with the truth? Could anyone else?

Jimmy drives home. Lloyd Klumpp is still yacking in his head. Jimmy can't concentrate enough to understand the words. When he pulls into his driveway, he sees his dad back by the pigs. Jimmy stops short of the back porch, unzips his "barn door" and pees in the snow—trying unsuccessfully to write fuck you!

When he goes into the house his ma's in the kitchen. Jimmy stops for one second and looks at the back of her head while she stands at the sink peeling potatoes. "Where you been?" she asks. He wants her to hug him, but that's not possible. It might make him sick. He slips past her, bounds up the stairs to his room. It's miserable cold upstairs all winter. There's no direct heat up there—only what finds its way up the stairway.

Jimmy runs into the room and flops onto his bed. "I will . . . not . . . blubber . . . like a fuckin' . . . baby," he mutters with his face in his pillow, blubbering.

Eleven

Jimmy pulls into the school parking lot just as bus number twelve begins to unload. It's Monday. He doesn't know why he came. He skipped his last class on Thursday and all day Friday. Maybe he should go on skipping. They haven't called his house yet. He isn't interested in anything that's happening in this fucking place. It doesn't have anything to do with life. He's not going to college or any place else. Sumpter will pick on him in gym again today, make him gather up the balls after class or some other stupid thing while all of the other guys go to the showers. Pretty soon he's going to lose it and nail that fucker, even if he is a teacher.

Tap, tap, tap. Jimmy turns his head to see the prettiest girl in school tapping on his window. "Where were you yesterday?" Starr snarls at him. He rolls down the window. She leans in to rest her books on the opening. "My dad caught me hanging out in the woods at the side of the road waiting for you. Where were you?" Her voice was screechy and loud. "And then he unplugged my phone, took it out of my room, nailed my windows shut and made me stay in there until this morning. God, can you believe it? Where were you?"

Jimmy picks up a pack of cigarettes sitting on the seat beside him. "Care for a smoke," Jimmy says, calmly, as he holds the pack out for her. Starr looks disgusted. She stands up straight. One of her books falls to the pavement as

165

the bell rings behind her. Starr grabs the book and rushes off looking like she's just experienced a street bum trying to put the make on her. She saw him differently. Jimmy could see it in her face. She saw him for the first time as others have seen him all along. Jimmy looks at the pack of cigarettes and thinks, she's gone, lost. He's lost his Starr.

Jimmy knew he wasn't going to school today when he pulled in. Today's the day! Jimmy decides. He starts his car. Today the shit hits the fan. Many heads turn as *Dack Dick's* Indy 500 car lays rubber as it screeches out of the parking lot. In reality *Jimmy* sticks the pedal-to-the-metal and his New Yorker gimps out in jerks. No one is looking. Fuck you all he thinks. He actually gets his New Yorker up to forty by the time he passes Buddy's. Then he has to slow down to turn onto Roundtree. But he barely makes the turn before he steps on the pedal again to propel his speeding bullet on down to Charlie Yates's farm. He's tired of fucking around with all of this shit. "The shit will hit the fan," Dack announces.

Jimmy doesn't turn into the driveway at Charlie's farm. Instead he yanks the steering wheel to the right *after* the driveway and heads his Chrysler across the yard between two big trees toward the house. The car does a major slowdown as soon as it hits the pile of plowed snow at the edge of the road. The shit will hit the fan, he keeps thinking. Jimmy's holding the wheel as tightly as he can, bracing himself for impact. Snow sprays onto the windshield blinding him as the steering wheel wrenches his hands off it with a sudden, strong turn to the left. The car keeps going but Jimmy's not at the steering wheel. He's been thrown to the floor on the passenger side. This is it, Jimmy thinks. He feels peaceful, serene, like he sometimes does out at the cemetery.

Finally the car sputters off and stops dead. Jimmy lays on the floor for a minute, stunned. Then he opens the passenger side door and looks around. Jimmy Trueberry's done a big circle in Charlie Yates's front yard. "Ah, maaaaan," he says. "I did a big fuckin' donut."

Jimmy's pissed. Jimmy's real pissed. With the door hanging open, he walks away, rubbing his right shoulder. The front door of the house looks like nobody's been in or out of it in years. The bushes have taken it over. Jimmy finds the back door to the enclosed porch. A terrified looking cat races from behind the freezer, out an opening and across the snow to the barn. Jimmy opens the porch door and stomps to the inner door. He pounds on it, rattling panes in the porch windows.

Fuck! He ain't home, Jimmy finally decides. He looks around on the porch. "Reedville Woman Megabucks Winner," the *Citizen-Times* announces on top of the freezer. A puked-up hair ball lay right next to it on top of some other papers. Jimmy's fingers reach out to touch a gray jacket hanging from a hook on the wall. It's scratchy. He lifts the jacket off the hook and looks down at it as he holds it in both of his hands. He doesn't see anything more than a gray jacket, but it's Charlie Yates's gray jacket. He's touching Charlie Yates's scratchy gray jacket. Don't ask him why, but he holds it close to him.

In front of him a cardboard box of folded paper grocery bags sits on top of another bigger box filled with *Reader's Digests*. Charlie's *Reader's Digests*. Jimmy thinks Charlie probably reads them while he sits in a recliner with a window on one side and a floor lamp on the other. Two old fishing poles stand in the corner. Jimmy wonders if Charlie uses them both or if someone fishes with him—someone who keeps their pole here? On the floor along the end wall is a row of men's boots—a pair of knee highs flopped over with bits of dried manure stuck on the black rubber and some dusty work boots in various states of wear, one pair caked with mud.

Jimmy is standing on Charlie Yates's back porch looking at his stuff, bits of Charlie Yates. Things he uses, touches, wears. This stuff belongs to his . . . Jimmy doesn't know what to call him. Is he his *first* dad? His *other* dad? His *real* dad? He's his "some-kinda" dad. Jimmy is bewildered. He looks out the windows behind him. His house is back there beyond the woods which obscures the view. He can about guess where it is on the other side of the trees. While he gazes that way, the subtle shape of the cabin halfway between here and home comes into focus.

Jimmy's got to do something about his car in the front yard. His Chrysler is in Charlie Yates's front yard packed underneath with a heavy, wet snow. His dad's going to kill him. Who knows what Charlie Yates will do? Probably the same thing since he's his dad, too. Jimmy's fighting a strong urge to put two fingers in his mouth and suck.

Instead, Jimmy decides to walk home to get the tractor. Maybe he can get his car pulled out before Charlie gets home. Maybe no one will notice it before he can get it pulled out of there. If someone sees it in the yard, he's a gonner. Everybody around here is always yacking about everybody else. Everybody is always into everybody else's business. They're all a bunch of yackers who can't keep their mouths shut. They report on each other all of the time—all of them.

Jimmy's already cold as he walks to the lane. Charlie's big boot prints are still visible under a light snow that fell since Charlie last walked back here. Someone with smaller feet has walked down here, too. It must have been his fuckin' ma coming to fuck her *boyfriend*. He's feeling repulsed. Jimmy puts his feet where Charlie's feet walked. It makes him feel funny. It makes him feel like a stupid little kid—the kind of little kid who thinks his dad is cool.

Jimmy's nose is running. He uses his sleeve to wipe it. His feet are freezing cold. He turns to look back at Charlie's house to see what it looks like from near the cabin. The big white farmhouse looms up out of the white snow. The red barn to the right looks like it's smiling because of the way the doors have been trimmed in white. Jimmy thinks it looks like the picture on the front of a Christmas card.

He shoves his hands deep into his pockets and walks on. He's having to go past that cabin. His shoulders are bunched up around his neck. Jimmy consciously doesn't look at the cabin as he walks by. He's feeling okay, calm. He needs to get the tractor over there to Charlie Yates's and pull that car out of his yard. That's all he thinks about. It's not likely Jimmy can get out of this jam, but a big part of him doesn't really care. He's ready to do what has to be done, to face whatever happens. For the first time in his life, he feels ready to face whatever happens. He feels like he's been running for a long time. And Jimmy's tired of running.

****

Lizzie walks faster than the others to the women's lounge. When she gets there, she pulls off her hairnet and puts on her coat. She's already on her way out the door when LaShonda opens it. "Where you goin', girl?" LaShonda asks. Lizzie doesn't answer. She has fifteen minutes to get to a pay phone, do her business and get back to work. She drives straight to the Marathon station on Pearl Street where you can sit in your car to use the phone.

Lizzie's side mirror almost scrapes the corner of the phone box as she pulls up to it. She already checked to make sure she had the change. She turns her coin purse upside down into a rectangular indentation on top of the dash that must be for holding things like change. For years its been holding Lizzie's gum and wrappers. She drops in two dimes and then dials. The phone rings and rings. No one answers. Lizzie hangs up. Her dimes clatter into the return box. She takes them out and tries again. The kids from a nearby grade school are walking home for lunch. A boy across the street makes a snowball and throws it to this side, trying to hit a girl in a hot pink hat as she walks by Lizzie's car. It misses and hits her car as Lizzie sits there listening to endless rings. The boy runs down the street as the girl screams at him. The phone must have rung fifty times before Lizzie is able to hang up.

Something is wrong. Something is terribly wrong. She couldn't get him last night when she called at nine-thirty. When she tried at ten-ten, there was still no answer. None at ten-twenty or twenty-one, two or three. At ten-thirty, she let it ring for five minutes before she hung up. At eleven, she convinced herself that the phone was out of order. She put on her coat and boots and walked to his house. She didn't care about footprints. That didn't even enter her mind. She *always* calls on Sunday night. No matter what, she *always* calls. He *always* answers on Sunday night. *Always*—no exceptions! He didn't answer last night and he wasn't home. His car was in the garage, but the house was unlocked. He wasn't there. He wasn't at the cabin because there was no smoke coming out of the chimney. That's how she knows if he's at the cabin in winter.

Lizzie flashes to when they found Eugene's father in the orchard. The flies were already buzzing around him. Lizzie starts to cry. Charlie may be laying in the snow, freezing to death. She's got to find him.

****

Steve told his secretary that he needed to tackle some complicated paperwork that would take all of his concentration. He told her he had decided to go home to do it. Now he's sitting at the breakfast nook looking out at the backyard birdfeeder. Several Jays have taken it over. The other birds are out in the trees waiting for an opportunity to

170

swoop in and grab a morsel. Once in a while one bravely makes it.

Steve shoves half a bagel with cream cheese into his mouth. He's got a big cavern of a mouth. He can and does get a lot in there in one bite. As his teeth pulverize, he remembers Cindy's cracking jaw. Whenever he's not occupied with something else Cindy pops into his mind. It's like that, a popping up, like a jack-in-the-box. Sometimes it even startles him. That's why he stays so busy—that and because he needs to make money.

No one has ever gotten under his skin the way that woman did. He's been real good these last few months, but lately Steve feels weak. He wants to be with her again. He admits that, finally. Yes. He wants to be with her again. That doesn't mean he will. Steve Gillette didn't get to where he is today without discipline. He's got discipline to spare. And he knows what he wants. He wants to be a millionaire and he's almost there and nothing is going to screw that up. He's wanted to be a millionaire since he was a kid and even now that millionaires aren't all that rare, he is determined. Who knows? Once he's there he may try for multimillionaire.

Steve picks bagel from his teeth as he remembers the first time he ever heard of Cynthia Wickett Mead. He had seen her paintings at an exhibit that Joan had dragged him to in Ann Arbor. They were with another couple who were such bores that he'd decided to spice up the outing. Cindy's work was the most outlandish in the exhibit. And knowing how rigid Joan can be in her judgment of what is art, Steve had decided to start *making* over Cindy's work to embarrass Joan in front of her boring friends from the college.

He'd picked Cindy's painting of a reclining nude with big red lips. On her bare belly was a gathering of dancing mice looking like they were having a hoedown complete with checkered kerchiefs around the necks of some and flouncey, square dance skirts on others. The nude was smoking a cigarette and had blown a big blue cloud of smoke over the heads of the mice.

Steve had struck a pose in front of the painting which was titled, "Mouse Dancers #3." He'd rubbed his chin between his thumb and first finger. He had stood there for a while wondering if they'd ever notice that he wasn't cruising the gallery with them and like them, making inane comments. He moved on to another of Cindy's paintings. Finally, Joan's heels had curtly clicked across the big room with James and Marcia trailing behind.

"Steve," Joan had inquired, "what are you doing?"

Steve didn't answer. By that time he had truly become absorbed in Cindy's paintings. He had noticed how sad the nude looked and that out the window a tiny nude man, who could easily be missed, was on a tiny step ladder off in the distance, on top of a hill looking every bit like he was hanging a crescent moon in a deep purple sky. Steve had wondered what that meant, what the blue hair meant, what the fountain pen meant with red ink running like a river out of it across the floor beside the nude. He'd never really looked at art this closely before. He'd never seen anything that interested him enough. He probably wouldn't have seen this if he hadn't been working up to one of his passive-aggressive jabs at Joan.

"Steve," Joan had announced in her pleasant voice that she puts on to pretend she's not bothered, "we're ready to go. We *have* to go. We have reservations at the Gandy Dancer for seven."

"I don't give a royal shit," Steve had barked back. "I'm busy!"

Joan looked like she could have died. She was so embarrassed. "Look at this," Steve had snapped as he waved them over closer. "Look at this guy out the window. What do you think that means?" James and Marcia bent over for a closer look.

"I think it means that the artist whomever it is . . . ," Joan stated condescendingly as she searched for a name on the card on the wall. "I think it means that Cynthia Wickett Mead can't conceive, compose or execute a painting very well." She laughed prompting Marcia to laugh with her.

Steve had taken his eyes off the painting for the first time in several minutes. Exchanging places it was *he* who had glared at *Joan* and then he had continued to stroll around looking at each of Cindy's paintings—five in the exhibit. He'd asked the gallery attendant to give him information on the artist. She gave him a copy of Cindy's resume and one of her artist statement while Joan telephoned the restaurant twice to tell them they were going to be fifteen minutes late.

"Steven, hurry up," Joan had admonished as though he were a child she was dressing for school. Steve took his time and it wasn't to *get* Joan. It was because he'd become fascinated by Cindy's art. Cindy had revealed so much about herself to him through her paintings, but he had no idea what she'd revealed. He knew that didn't make sense. He felt as though he'd seen her soul—that's how he put it to Cindy.

When he'd told Joan that Cynthia Wickett Mead lives in Reed County, Joan had stated flatly, knowingly, "It figures. There aren't any good artists in Reed County." She'd said it right in front of the gallery worker who may have been the owner because she looked insulted.

Steve had called Cindy the next Monday and said he wanted to buy a painting. He'd rather get it directly from her because that way she wouldn't have to share the profit with the gallery owner who is probably the wife of some rich guy who needs a "fulfilled" wife and a tax write-off. Steve said that he figured gallery owners are well-to-do and *being an artist must be a struggle.* That statement right there had instantly endeared him to Cindy. She'd told him later that she couldn't believe how perceptive he was to her plight as an artist. Eventually she had likened them to Katherine Hepburn and Spencer Tracy and like them, there were great differences, but an undeniable bond and passion. They both confessed that neither of them felt it before.

Steve sighs, shakes his head and gulps some milk directly from the jug. Things got bad around here yesterday. He had driven to get this milk at around two-thirty. Joan and Starr had forgotten to get it when they went to the store earlier. Steve had volunteered to go just so he could get out of the house.

When he went around the bend beyond their drive he happened to glance to his right and saw Starr back in the woods. Joan had just informed him that Starr was in her room taking a nap. In fact Joan had yelled at him to be quiet when he bellowed out of the bathroom asking who'd been using his straightedge?

When Starr had seen Steve's car she ran deeper into the woods. Probably to hide herself better. If she'd stayed put there's a chance he might not have seen her at all. When Steve stopped his car Starr had taken off running between the trees toward the house. Steve was about to explode. It was an impulsive reaction, like the one he'd had when Starr was born and he ran out of the hospital into the rain and ran for about ten blocks, yelling that he'd just had a baby.

Steve turned his car around in the Simpson's driveway. He didn't know what Starr was up to but it wasn't anything good—anybody could tell that. That kid has a long way to go to be as slick as her dad. He could have come up with a dozen explanations if he were in her situation. But the first thing he would have done is to stay put. When you run— you're guilty—even if you're not.

If Steve were in Starr's place, he would have said, "Mother must have misunderstood what I was doing" or "I *did* take a nap and now I'm doing something for school. I have to get some dried leaves for an art project" or "I have to get some winter plant samples for science" or "I'm writing a short story for English and I had to come out here to get the feeling of what it would be like for a Native American from the seventeen hundreds to suddenly discover a paved road with cars." Then he'd act enthused and ask, "Can you imagine what it would be like to be a primitive person discovering the world as it is today?" Hell, Steve could have come up with a dozen excuses. He hears trumped-up excuses every day from his suppliers and employees.

Starr had run for the house and reached it just as he pulled into the driveway. Steve slammed his car in park, didn't even take the keys out or turn the car off for that matter. He was possessed as he ran in after her. They both had raced past Joan. When Starr had reached her room, she slammed the door and locked it. *This time* Steve lost it. He'd thrown his shoulder against the door trying to break it down, like in the movies, but the first blow had about broken his shoulder. He'd run to the tool chest in the garage to get some tools to remove the door hinges. Of course the whole time he was yelling at Starr to come out.

Joan had recovered from an impending catatonic coma long enough to tell Steve that she had seen Starr run past the great room windows. Steve dropped the hammer and screw driver and flew out the front door. Starr jumped into his car and was starting to back it down the driveway despite the fact that she hadn't even started driver's training and it showed the way she was weaving from one edge of the plowed drive to the other. Steve had known he couldn't get himself to the driver's side at the speed she was going and that the passenger side was locked, so he'd thrown himself on the hood of the car. That must have scared Starr because when she heard the thump she turned around from looking behind the car to the front where Steve's eyes were riveted to hers through the windshield.

Starr had screamed, slammed on the brakes, opened her door, jumped out and had run for the house. The car was still going in reverse but slower. Shit, Steve wasn't about to let his hot-shot baby get wrecked. He had barely managed to get in there and get the thing stopped before it had entered the road. Steve silently thanked Joan for the long driveway on which she had insisted.

" . . . but that was yesterday and yesterday's gone," Steve sings to himself as he puts the milk jug away and notices some bagel crumbs floating on the surface. Joan will have a fit when she sees that. So be it, he thinks, not even considering trying to get them out. In the past he'd be fishing around in there trying to get the crumbs out. No more! He lives here, too, god damn it! He's tired of pussyfooting around Joan. She's going to have to learn to live with a crude, inconsiderate *man* or else go find herself a cultured, catering *woman*. Those are her choices as far as Steve can figure out.

Steve stands before the sliding glass window off the breakfast nook, with his hands on his hips. Joan has classes all afternoon. Starr's at school until three. He looks at the phone. Cindy asked him to call today.

****

Cindy is having a bad, bad day. She can't paint. She can't write. She can't do anything but cry and pace the floor. She's feeling so lonely. Why does Rita Spurr think she has such a great life? Can't they see what she has given up to have what she has? She'd convinced them all that she had the greatest life on earth. She'd convinced herself, but she has given up the cherished illusion and god forbid, now she has to reveal to the family of man that that is exactly what it was. Illusions are a way of life in the Wickett family. The unspoken Wickett code of conduct decrees that if you're going to reveal any truthful feelings you might as well run down Main Street naked and get it over with. Keep yourself in a blinding fog! Keep everyone else in a blinding fog! The family motto: We're OKAY! We're OKAY! We're OKAY, Okay?

Cindy feels naked. She wishes she was naked. Naked with Steve in room five or anywhere—even sprawled across the center line of Main Street . . . in a snowstorm . . . at rush hour (which is from five to five-fifteen when the Reedville City and Reed County employees get out).

Cindy wants to call Steve, but Mrs. Lowe would be the one to answer. Cindy believes that Mrs. Lowe was onto Cindy and Steve. It's humiliating the way Edith Lowe tried to run interference. She would say, "May I ask who is calling?" Cindy is certain that Edith recognizes her voice. But Cindy is always forced to announce, like a child confessing: "This is Cynthia Wickett Mead, the artist." Then, Edith would say, "Just a moment, please, I'll see if Mr. Gillette is available." Cindy would condescendingly be put on hold.

Cindy imagines Edith going to the bathroom or typing another paragraph before she buzzes Steve. Sometimes she comes back to say in her clippy style, "Mrs. Mead are you still there? I'm sorry! I had another call after yours and it took a while to finish. I'll buzz Mr. Gillette, now." It makes Cindy feel like a slut and she's not. But, in the past, if she'd been in Mrs. Lowe's position, she would have done the same thing to her boss's slut.

Cindy plops down on her bed. The pink polish on her toenails is chipping. She kept all of her nails perfect for a year. Now that Cindy is depressed and dysfunctional her nails look awful. She's got a rich client in Bloomfield Hills over by Detroit, who wants Cindy to bring her paintings to her house, but she can't make herself return the call.

Cindy has convinced herself that Steven Gillette never cared for her. That she was merely a diversion to take his mind off his miserable marriage for a while. She wouldn't want to get mixed up with herself either if she were Steve. What could she possibly offer him? She's no match for Joan. Joan's the mother of his child. The cook of all cooks. The culture queen of Reedville society. Joan's a mature woman of good breeding. Cindy's a child who refuses to grow up. She's the artist not the patron. She belongs in a garret not a manor. And her thighs are riddled with deep, dark caverns on the back.

Steve's not going to call as she asked him to yesterday. She knows he won't call. Tonight Cindy will tell Bruce that she is leaving him. Tomorrow she will have Merryweather put to death, it's time, she's not holding her food down. She's skin and bones. It's past time. Cindy doesn't want to do it. She's still grieving over all of the other old pets she hauled in to have put to death . . . and Marilyn. She's still grieving for Marilyn. She will move into the extra bedroom and when she can get her act together Cindy will be out of there too. It's past time. She'll leave without another word to Steve. She'll vanish. Poof!

****

Three cars have gone by since Jimmy got the tractor attached by a chain to his car. One of the drivers slowed down to gawk. Charlie Yates still isn't home. It doesn't matter. Jimmy's probably been "caught" by somebody in one of those cars who will *yack* about it.

Jimmy shoveled as much snow as he could out from under the car and now he's ready to try to pull it with the tractor. He pulls up the gas lever, let's out on the clutch and feels the car give a little. He has the tractor in low gear and its tires are on the plowed driveway. Just as he gets ready to give it more gas, his ma pulls in. Man, these gossips work fast, Jimmy thinks.

Elizabeth can hardly believe what she is seeing. "Jimmy, what's your car doin' over there?" she yells above the tractor engine.

Jimmy puts the clutch back in, takes it out of gear, pulls up the brake. He turns the key and the tractor sputters off. "Ma, I don't want to talk about it right now. I just wanna get my car out."

Elizabeth doesn't want to talk about it either. *He knows,* she thinks. She feels it in her gut. Her heart begins to pound in her chest like something awful has happened. In a minute or so she'll feel an overwhelming rush of energy and anxiety. Someone at work told her that is what is called a "fight or flight reaction." Elizabeth doesn't want to do either one. She wants her son to be at school. She wants Charlie to be in the house in his easy chair. And she wants it to be six months from now.

"Jimmy, is Charlie Yates home?" She looks up at Jimmy on the tractor.

He doesn't ask her why she wants to know. He just says, "No."

"Have you seen him, today?"

"No." That's all he says. His ma looks small down there—and scared. Her eyes are real big.

"Jimmy, I think . . . something is wrong with Charlie Yates. I need to look for him," she says cautiously. She starts to move around the tractor, slowly, walking toward the house.

After she gets halfway to the house, Jimmy yells, "Ma—do you want some help?"

Elizabeth stops, but she doesn't turn around. Her shoulders had jumped a little when he spoke. She answers, "Please."

Jimmy gets down, walks over to her. Her head is bent down. She's pretty small, his ma, even from down here. They walk to the house. "I'm going to look upstairs," she says as they enter the back porch. She doesn't look to see what Jimmy thinks of that. "Charlie," she yells as she stomps her feet on the rug in front of the kitchen door. Jimmy does it, too. "You look all around downstairs. Don't miss anything. Look in the closets. Look for signs—anything suspicious. I'm afraid something terrible has happened," she says to Jimmy. "Charlie," she yells again, heading up the stairs.

Jimmy's alarmed at what his mother is suggesting. What if his dad found out and killed Charlie? What if Jimmy opens a closet and finds the bloody corpse? What if Charlie *is* dead?

When they find no one in the house including the basement and attic and nothing in the barn, garage or any of the other outbuildings, Elizabeth goes back to the porch to put on Sarah's boots. She calls Jimmy in to put on a pair of Charlie's heavy insulated boots. He sits in the metal lawn chair on the back porch, takes off his wet socks and shoes. Neither one of them says a thing. Elizabeth brings him a dry pair of Charlie's socks from inside the house. Jimmy places Charlie's gray jacket over the shoulders of his mother's winter coat. He doesn't want her to get cold.

They both troop around in the fields behind the house for about an hour. Jimmy checks the drainage ditches. Finally, Jimmy says, "What about the shack?"

"I don't think he'd be there," Elizabeth responds while wiping her nose with a raggedy Kleenex from her pocket. "There would have been smoke . . . " she stops before mentioning last night.

"We should look," Jimmy says already starting that way and thinking about those tracks in the snow—realizing that they only went one direction.

When he gets there he notices the lantern on the porch. Elizabeth is right behind him. "Oh," she says in an exhale of breath that clouds her face. "Jimmy don't go in there!" Jimmy has already started to open the door. Elizabeth hides her eyes and turns her back as the door cries out.

Jimmy can't move. He can't feel. He can't speak. He can't puke. Did Jimmy die after all? No, no, the blue man has. Jimmy's stiff, blue "some-kinda" dad is dead.

Twelve

The trillium has finished blooming. The woods is turning yellow-green again. Elizabeth watches the people across the field swarm Charlie's house and barnyard. They look like squirrels gathering nuts, carrying things around. This is her last pilgrimage to the cabin, at least for a while. The only reason she's here now is because of the auction. She and Jimmy couldn't stop the auction, but Jimmy's lawyer is trying to freeze the proceeds as well as stop the sale of the property. Jimmy has a lawyer who in front of God and everybody in Reed County and the State of Michigan is attempting to establish paternity which would make Jimmy Charlie's rightful heir. They're using her diaries and some love notes Charlie wrote her as evidence that Charlie claimed Jimmy as his own—that Jimmy was carefully planned—so there would be no mistake. Eugene may be forced into taking a blood test to rule him out.

Lizzie doesn't understand this part. The lawyer said something about a scientific test that might require them to dig up Charlie's body and take a sample of his rib cage. If it comes to that Elizabeth knows Charlie wouldn't fault her. She messed up when he was alive. She doesn't want to mess up any more.

Elizabeth kicks at a rock as she stands in front of the little cabin. She heaves an involuntary sigh. She steps onto the little porch and pushes the door open with her hand. There they are right in front of her eyes—all of those years. All of the precious moments stolen from an unhappy marriage. The day when she realized that she loved the older farmer who lived behind her. The time she and Charlie made the decision to have a child together against all that she believed was moral. The many times he begged her to leave Eugene and tell Jimmy about fated love.

Elizabeth runs her hand across the sill of the window through which she first saw the man who would line her life, the way a garment's interfacing supports the outer fabric at the least stable points. It would be impossible to go on without him. That's what she believed to be true. She thought it would be impossible to give Jimmy the details of a story he thought he knew. She assumed it would be impossible to change her life, to leave Eugene, to face the community, the church, her god. But she did them all. Her life went on, too late to include Charlie.

Someone has taken the iron potbelly stove to the house to sell at the auction, leaving the stovepipe dangling from the ceiling. Her Charlie lay right there on that bed. That's where her precious Charlie died. Where life gobbled another huge chunk of Elizabeth.

Jimmy comes around the corner. He had walked back to see Eugene. "Dad don't look too good," Jimmy tells her, "and the house is a mess." Elizabeth pretends she doesn't hear by giving no response. She misses the nature—the quiet—the sense of being some place familiar. Yes, she does feel compassion for Eugene—enough so that she cannot let herself think about him.

She and Jimmy are taking a trip as soon as school is out. They're going to Arizona. Neither one of them has been out of the Midwest. They've only been in three states: Michigan, Indiana and Ohio. Will is trying to arrange it with his job in Indiana so he can go West too. Elizabeth has been praying for that to happen. They want to see cactus growing higher than their heads!

183

"Let's get back to the house, Jimmy. They'll be starting the household goods soon. Rose will be wondering where we are." Rose wants to bid on the pie safe that was in Charlie's kitchen. It was Charlie's mother's. Elizabeth will try for as much of the family memorabilia as she can afford for Jimmy—the Yates's bible and Grandpa Yates's farm diary with a detailed record of goods bought and sold and the daily weather. There's an entry in it about rigging the sleigh up to go to a dance in the grange hall, the one over on Pitch Road, and an entry recording the death of Charlie's uncle Thadeus of pneumonia when he was fifteen. Charlie showed Elizabeth the tattered little book several years ago.

Elizabeth puts her arm around Jimmy's waist as they walk the lane together. It feels awkward to her to be so openly affectionate. Her people caress their very young, weaning them away from their arms by the time they're three or four. By the time they're five or six they're alienated from parental physical affection, starved for a touch. The parents view any touching of children as unnatural. Except an hostile touch—that's natural.

Jimmy is a full head taller than Elizabeth. She can't believe that this big kid is her baby. The two of them are getting by, but it's tight with rent and all. She hasn't done anything about a divorce yet and Eugene would never start it. He wants her back.

As they get to the edge of the yard Jimmy sees Cindy Mead digging into a box of quilt blocks. "I'll see you later, ma," he says, "I wanta circulate."

Cindy's hair is pulled into a pony tail, held by a barrette. She is carrying a closed umbrella. She thinks it might sprinkle. You never can tell—no matter what they say on the acu-weather report. As she looks around she can't believe how many people haven't realized that it might sprinkle. It's stupid to bring an umbrella and then leave it in the car—

if that's what they've all done. The way these spring showers come on these people would be wet by the time they got to the car. Cars are lined up on both sides of the road for a half-mile. Cindy wonders if the auctioneers have plastic tarps ready to throw over things in case it rains. She wonders what they will do if there is a wind with it? How will they keep the tarps in place?

Cindy layer-dressed. You never know. If it gets warmer as the day goes on, she can remove one layer at a time. First the nylon rain poncho. Then the cotton blend jacket. Then the sweater. She can tie them one by one around her waist, so her hands will be free.

"Cindy Mead," Jimmy says as Cindy shifts her shoulder bag to the other shoulder. Glass bangs together inside. She's got two bottles of pop in there—in case they're still here when it's time. It's too expensive at the lunch wagon and Bruce doesn't like fountain pop. He thinks the fizz is better with the metal caps that have to be popped off with an opener which Cindy carries too—all the time. She knows Bruce is right about the fizz in the glass bottles. The plastic bottles aren't as healthy as glass. Bruce heard that somewhere. And you can't get enough volume in a can—only twelve ounces.

"Hi, Jimmy," Cindy says, stiffly. She looks frightened. "How are you doing—with Charlie's death and all? I'm sorry I never got the story written but a lot has happened in my life since I last saw you. I got a job for one thing—selling advertising for the *Citizen-Times*. I'm hoping to work into being a copywriter or layout artist. It's not great money but it's steady and that's what's needed in these times, steady income. So, how's school?"

"Perty good!" Jimmy tells her as a man walks up behind Cindy.

"We'd better go," the man snaps. "It's almost noon. We need to get home for lunch. Give me a pop." Cindy removes a bottle and unpops the lid.

"What about the tractor?" Cindy asks him.

"I'm not waiting around for that. Who knows when they'll auction it? Auctions are too unpredictable anyway. Besides, it's time to eat." The man walks away, never acknowledging Jimmy. Cindy says, apologetically, "I'd better go or I'll miss my ride. Then I'll have to walk home. Good-bye, Jimmy." Cindy holds her hand out. She feels she should make peace. Jimmy gives her his hand, but it makes him feel terrible. It's the hand that pulled the trigger on her Marilyn.

Cindy walks away holding her stomach. She's been having terrible pains lately. She's worried that it's stomach cancer. Cancer runs in her family. Bruce is always warning her about her diet. He has predicted that she'll have colon cancer because she doesn't have the right bathroom habits. Bruce has a specific time every day that he uses the bathroom and he tries to keep his stools the proper consistency by controlling his diet on a day by day basis. His menu is based on the consistency of his stools the day before. Cindy and Bruce both know that if she gets colon cancer, it will be her own fault. She's been warned plenty of times.

Cindy stops in the studio when they get home. Bruce keeps on going, asking, "When are you going to clean up this mess?" The door slams behind him before she can answer. He has to get the Campbell's split pea soup started. It's Saturday. She knows that! She knows she's made Bruce late.

Cindy has consolidated her studio into half of the space. Bruce figures that he ought to have half of it for his hobbies, too. He's building a wall right down the middle. He told Cindy she will still have room to do her hobby on the weekends, if she gets the house cleaned first. He's turning his side into a bullet reloading workshop. He reloads twenty-two's and makes lead balls for his muzzle loaders—one ball at a time. He's moving it out of the other side of the basement where it never should have been because of the table saws, band saw, sanders, drills and other tools that kick up dust.

Cindy sits on the chair at her drawing table and looks at the upright two-by-fours that divide her studio. He'd *asked* her if it would be all right to take half. He'd *hugged* her when he asked. He's *very considerate* of her. He *loves* her. Cindy has no doubt about that, Bruce loves her. He takes good care of her. He's the one who built this studio several years ago. Whenever she's depressed about her life, he's always right there to hug her, tell her that he'll take care of her. How many women would die to hear that?

Marilyn's dead! There's a dirty, red dog collar in a plastic bag on the table in front of her. Cindy doesn't know what to do with it, where to put it. It has been laying there for months. It showed up one day in January in their mailbox down on the road. The tag was still legible. "Marilyn . . . Cindy Mead . . . 8605 Meek Road . . . Reedville, MI" There was a note with it, scratches on a piece of lined paper torn out of a spiral bound notebook:

> *Yor dog is dead. I am sorry. It was fast. She didn't suffer. I am sorry cause I know she was too yung to die. Sorry.*

Cindy knows it was written by someone *"not no good with words."*

Cindy hears the radio upstairs. The waistband on her jeans is driving her crazy. She unsnaps and unzips a little and pulls her sweater down over it. She's growing out of her *fat* pants. She's not pregnant unless God chose her for his second child. It's driving her crazy, but she can't seem to

187

get a grip on her eating, and she can't stay with a diet anymore. Cindy walks over to her stash in a cardboard box covered by her palette and gets a Snickers. She can't get the wrapper off fast enough. Oh, God, she thinks, I needed this. She moans with ecstasy as she gnaws on it. A brown drool runs out the corner of her mouth.

****

"There's a letter from Starr on the counter," Joan advises Steve. It's past noon and he's just gotten out of bed. He always did sleep late on Saturday morning, but it's later than ever these days. Joan has already been to aerobics class and the nursery to pick up the Japanese iris for the pond. This year she's adding a footbridge with a hand-carved troll under it and a better kettle heater in one cove to keep the goldfish alive next winter. Next summer: the waterfall.

Joan's still in her exercise clothes. Joan's lost that little tummy and now she's working on upper body sculpting at the fitness center. Steve hasn't noticed. He hasn't approached her for nearly two years. Neither one of them mentions it. Joan does discuss it with her therapist. She tells Elaine everything.

"Money! Money! Money!" Steve says. "Is that all Starr can write about—how much *money* everybody comes from at that place? I don't think she should be going home for weekends with those girls. She's going to turn into an elitist snob with all of this money worship."

"It's a great school! We're lucky they took her midyear. Starr's getting a wonderful education and becoming a lovely young lady," Joan says as she unloads the dishwasher. "What more could we want? Look at the photo she sent! You can see her face without all of that makeup. Isn't she adorable? She looks so cute in that plaid skirt and blazer. Good thing there aren't any boys around there, they'd be all over her."

"Christ, she always sounds like she's ashamed of where she comes from," he says looking at the pink, perfumed paper. "This isn't any dump," Steve says as he looks around. "Maybe we should have named it something pretentious, so she can say she lives at *Gillette Grande* or *Reedville Country Manor.*

"You're making a mountain out of a mole hill as usual," Joan snaps at him as she throws the coffee maker grinds in the trash. Steve is insufferable to Joan. If she didn't have her little escapades to the Sheraton in Kalamazoo every three weeks, she'd be crazy by now. If she didn't have Mark to hold her tight, romance her, dance her, and you-know-what, she'd still be going to therapy *twice* a week. Does he really want Starr here—where she can see that trashy kid who made her lie and run all over the county at all hours of the day and night and who knows what else? (Starr refused to let a doctor examine her to verify she was *intact.*)

Steve Gillette looks at himself in the bathroom mirror. Does he look like a millionaire? He sure doesn't feel like a million bucks. He feels like shit. The truth is he isn't a millionaire and his dad is *dead.* He stood over that coffin at the funeral home, and when no one was in the room he bent over and kissed the old man on his cheek. It was the first affection that had ever passed between them as far as he could remember. Steve's starting to think that maybe the best he can expect with his life is to be *almost . . . almost a millionaire.*

After his dad died Steve agonized over what to do, how to proceed, since what he'd already been working so hard for could never happen. He finally decided by default to leave it alone, close his eyes and go on. He's too old to make any changes now. He's turning *fifty* this summer. Good god, he thinks, *fifty*. Nifty-Fifty as they put it in the classifieds when someone turns fifty. Friends will put a grade school or high school picture of a victim in the paper and above the picture it reads something like this: "Nifty! Nifty! Look who's turning FIFTY! Stop by Wolverine Color Printing and wish this *Stevie* another fifty!" Steve hopes to hell that no one does that to him. He wants it to pass unnoticed.

Cindy works at the paper now. Someone told him that. She may even be the one to lay out his unwanted Nifty-Fifty ad. That would be terrible. Steve hasn't seen her or talked to her for nearly five months. He still thinks about her. He looks at the painting all of the time. No one has any idea what's going through his head when he glances up at it as he passes by it. Sometimes when he's there after everyone has gone home, he'll wheel Edith's chair out from behind her desk, sit in it and gaze up at the painting with his feet on her desk. He must have been contented, rested and fulfilled when he knew Cindy.

On the painting she'd put an open door onto the side of his head with the number "5" on the door and the words "Escape For A View" floating out.

The border of the canvas is painted with fortune cookies going all of the way around. Once when they were picnicking in room five, Cindy, in a hokey, elaborate oriental ritual, offered Steve fortune cookies. One by one he opened them to discover the most profound fortunes. Things like: *Beware of business man in hot-shot car*—Cindy grabbed that one away from him and said, coyly "Why, that must have been mine." and . . . *You make love like a million bucks.* She assured him that was his. He finally caught on when he got the one that said, *With all her heart, Cindy Windy wuvs you.* She had pulled out all of the fortunes from the cookies and stuffed in her own which she'd typed and cut to look like the real thing.

190

Sometimes Steve gets the magnifying glass that he bought and keeps in his center desk drawer and steps up on Edith's chair to peer into the right eyeball in the painting. He and Cindy are the only ones who know that what looks like a highlight on his pupil is a tiny image of Cindy's face. She painted it with a three hair brush and a pair of special, lighted magnifying glasses.

Sometimes it's easier for Steve to forget her than at other times. When he's busy he never thinks of her. He's busy most of the time. You'd think in a town this size they'd run into each other somewhere. But they run in different circles. Still, he finds himself looking for her truck whenever he's out driving. And he plays the tapes that they both enjoyed—that were played a lot at the Tidy View. Those tapes really conjure up the feelings. Once in a while he'll drive by her house and peer up into the woods. *He had to let her go.* It simply wasn't meant to be. But Steve's been feeling lonely lately. He feels like he has nothing to look forward to but more busy—*more money.*

Starr's first dance will be at that school in Ohio. He hopes that someone will take photos and that Starr will send them home. She'll not be here when they receive her grades each marking period. Steve will call her and tell her how proud he is. He'll go on and on. He misses the spark that she gave this suddenly pretentious, dull house. It seems ridiculous to Steve to heat all of it all winter for two people. Steve had proposed to Joan in early February that they partition part of it off during the coldest months and not heat that part at all—like the great room, the dining room and maybe even the *entertainment* room. He said they could watch TV in the bedroom and he could move his desk from his home office into there. They could live in their bedroom, the kitchen and the bathroom off their bedroom—which together is more square footage than all of Steve's childhood home for a family of six.

And then Joan had asked, "What about the hall? Would it be heated or would we have to pull on our jackets to go from the bedroom to the kitchen?" She didn't wait for a response. She'd informed him immediately that she'd have nothing to do with even discussing it other than to say, "I don't care if it takes my whole years salary. I'm not living in a half-heated house like some redneck, ne'er-do-wells." She'd made Steve feel like the hick he'd left behind when they married twenty-some years ago. She'd made him feel like poor, white trash—the kind of people who could heat their house on what Steve pays in a year for electricity to illuminate the in-ground lights that line the sidewalk, to heat a spot in the lily pond for the goldfish in winter and to provide Steve's long soaks in the hot tub. Hell, yes, he's guilty of overconsumption too. But he admits it.

Steve is heading out to the deck soon. He's going to fire up the hot tub and destroy the earth with his decadence. He needs a good long soaking. But before he gets there Joan screams from the deck.

"What's wrong?" Steve yells out the window.

"God, there's a *rat* swimming in the hot tub! You idiot, you didn't put the cover on last night."

Steve runs out to find a furry thing swimming around and around. "That's not a rat, Joan," he says as he gets down on his knees. "It's a cat! For God's sake can't you tell a little cat from a rat?" It's hard for Steve to believe, sometimes, that this woman is college educated—let alone a college professor. "Help me out here!"

"What should I do?" Joan asks, helplessly wringing her hands as a way of not getting them wet.

"Oh, forget it!" Steve snarls as he kneels at the edge. He knows she doesn't want to get herself wet. "Come here, guy," he says as he reaches in and hauls out a very limp, worn-out rag-of-a-cat. "Get a towel, Joan," Steve commands. Even if it were a drowning rat, Steve would have tried to save it. He gave a bundle of money to the humane society for their proposed new shelter, and he stops now to move turtles off the road—turtles that he would have never even noticed a year-and-a-half ago. And he keeps his eye out for that little dog she lost—Cindy lost. Marilyn. He looks for Marilyn. Even though it has been a long time, Steve knows that she must still agonize over Marilyn's disappearance—what it would mean for her to discover that Marilyn hadn't been run over or starved to death or any of the other scenarios that terrorize her when her mind gets going.

Steve holds the drenched cat close to his chest to warm it up. The front of his robe is wet. Both he and the cat are dripping as he walks into the kitchen. He lays the cat on a dishtowel on the counter and grabs another one out of the drawer to wrap around it. The cat lets out a feeble little squeak. "You look like hell," Steve tells it softly, sensitive to the fact that she can't understand the words, only his tone. He can feel all of its bones. It's half-starved. Steve's used to feeling that two-ton ball-of-fat, Romeo, who lays around the house all day, year after year, eating and sleeping, peeing and pooping. This cat has been on its own for a while. Its fur is all matted. Steve lifts its tail to take a look at what's down under. No testicles or empty sacks. It's an upside down exclamation point, not a colon. Cindy taught him that, for sexing kittens. *It's a girl,* he announces loudly to Joan who's nowhere around. She's a little gray and white, long-haired, girl cat with *big green orbs* for eyes.

Steve rubs her body trying to dry her, trying to get some circulation going. Joan comes in with rag towels from the cleaning lady's supply closet. "Oh Steve look what you've done." She uses the towels to mop the floor. "Here," she says. "give me those kitchen towels. That's so unsanitary, Steve. Honestly!" She hands him two of the dry rag towels. It's hard for her to believe that this man can make that business thrive the way he does when he pulls something like this. That cat is probably diseased, Joan thinks. If it doesn't kill *us,* it will probably kill Romeo—*posthumously.* It looks half dead already.

Steve is determined that this cat survive. He grabs the phone. "Who's our vet?" he yells. He feels like he's in an emergency room dealing with a life or death situation.

"It's on the list on the wall. For god's sake," Joan says, walking away, "why don't you just call animal control and have them come out and pick it up?"

He gets an answering machine at the vets. "Yes, yes, this is an emergency. Call the Gillettes, Steven Gillette as soon as possible." He hangs up not thinking to speed it up by giving his phone number. He dials again without looking for any number.

"Who are you calling, now?" Joan asks bitchily as she passes through on her way to the laundry room, grabbing wet towels. She's gone before he can answer. The cat makes a meep sound and looks up at Steve.

"That's right, Pea Blossom," Steve murmurs, stroking her gently. The cat raises her head when she hears the sound "Blossom" and looks into Steve's eyes. The two of them connect in some nonverbal, species-to-species, primal way.

Steve reverts back to what he knows best, language, leaving Blossom to interpret. "Hang in there, honey. I'm going to help you out!"

The way he sounds and looks makes Blossom feel safe—safe from the water, safe from that harsh sound that swept through the room with that other being.

Steve listens as the the phone signals for Cindy at the other end. "Please be there," he beseeches.

Romeo plods into the kitchen. He senses, smells and then *sees* a stranger on his countertop—to which Romeo is too fat to ever even *think* about leaping. Romeo hisses! Pea Blossom lifts her head again and hisses back. She still feels safe, but instinctively she *displays* as much as she can by turning her big green orbs into slits and putting forth a feeble, little growl.

"Hey Romeo," Steve tosses down toward his big fat cat, "say hello to Juliet!" Romeo hisses again, looking more alert than he has in years.

"Hello?"

It's her! It's her, his pretty Cindy! "Hello, Cindy?" Steve says, very business like; but, with a youthful skip to his heartbeat.

Cindy wipes brown goo off her chin.

"This is Steve Gillette.   Listen, I've got a cat here in trouble."

Steve strokes Juliet.

"And . . . and I need you."

Juliet purrs into a roar.

The fat cat paces the Congoleum, trying to catch a scent, whiskers twitching, itching to get to Juliet.

RASPBERRY HILL PRESS
BOX 73
HORTON, MICHIGAN
49246

517-524-8909

$13.95 each. (add $3 shipping/handling <u>per</u> book)

# of Books _____

Michigan residents add $ .90 for state sales tax

Total enclosed_____

Name_____

Address_____

City/State/Zip_____

You may telephone orders using Visa or Mastercard.
517-524-8909

Please include the following:
1. Card Number
2. Cardholder's name
3. Expiration date
4. Shipping address
5. Phone number
6. Your calculation of the total charge.